WHEN OPPOSITES ATTRACT...

Darrin Mann knows what it's like to claw your way to the top. Growing up as the oldest of four with an absentee mother, Darrin worked his ass off to get out of the little three bedroom house he'd grown up in just outside of Beaumont.

Now a hotshot sports agent and Dallas' newly-crowned Most Eligible Bachelor, Darrin enjoys the finer things in life—expertly tailored Italian suits, the best wine money can buy, and the occasional perfectly coiffed woman.

There's just one problem—being crowned Dallas' Most Eligible Bachelor isn't all it's cracked up to be.

In an effort to escape the media and random, kind of creepy, pairs of panties being left on his doorstep and mailed to his office, Darrin decides to spend some time down at The Devils Ranch...where he meets single mom Miranda Jacobson, the most imperfectly coiffed woman imaginable.

What could Dallas' Most Eligible Bachelor and a wildlife biologist have in common?

More than they think...

By Aubrey Gross

Dallas' Most Eligible

AUBREY GROSS

Copyright

Book layout © 2016 Indie Book Design
Book cover © 2016 by Indie Book Design

Dallas' Most Eligible/Aubrey Gross -- 2nd ed.

Epub Edition September 2016 ISBN: 978-0-9981896-0-4

Print Edition ISBN: 978-0-9962821-9-2

To all the makeshift families out there. You're awesome.

CHAPTER ONE

What three qualities do you look for in a potential girl-friend?

THE MOMENT DARRIN MANN FOUND A PAIR OF PANTIES IN HIS MAIL was the moment he decided to get the hell out of Dodge.

To be fair, this wasn't the first pair of random panties he'd been gifted over the past month. These were by far the most outrageous, though, he thought as he lifted them out of the box they'd been shipped in.

Even though he rolled his eyes, he had to give the sender credit—the lacy red crotchless g-string was certainly inventive, if not a little unnecessary. What was the point of a crotchless g-string? Might as well wear nothing at all.

He sighed and threw them in the trash, along with the box they'd been shipped in. How these women kept getting his home address was beyond him, but the fan mail—so to speak—was getting ridiculous.

He padded over to the refrigerator and pulled out a locally brewed IPA before making his way to his home office. No sooner had he sat down than his cell vibrated in his back pocket.

He pulled it out and smiled when he saw the name on the screen.

"Hey, man. What's up?"

"Jenn's having a panic attack because you haven't RSVP'd yet. Do you really want to upset a pregnant woman?" his client and best friend Matt Roberts asked.

"Since I really like your future wife, no, I don't want to upset her. I've been trying to get a couple of contracts wrapped up before Spring Training ends and it's looking like that may not happen, along with prepping a couple of guys for the NFL draft. You know how crazy this time of year can be."

"Preaching to the choir, man."

He sat down in his desk chair and woke up his laptop. "I know. The wedding's this weekend, right?"

"Uh, yes."

"I feel like a shitty friend."

"Don't. Just try to be here. Hell, I'll even forgive you if you work a little while you're here."

Darrin laughed just as his doorbell rang.

"You need to get that?" Matt asked.

"Nope."

"Afraid it's another bachelorette on your doorstep?"

"Absolutely. It's getting ridiculous."

"You're the one who decided to do the Dallas' Most Eligible thing."

He ran a hand over his face as his doorbell rang again. "When they approached me I figured it could be good, harmless publicity. I didn't realize things would get so crazy."

Matt laughed. "You should've known things would get nutty, D. You're a reasonably attractive, highly successful single man with twenty-four seven access to pro athletes. Of course women are going to harass you."

The doorbell rang again. "Jesus," Darrin muttered as he got up to politely tell his unexpected visitor to go away. "Give me a second, Matt, whoever's at the door is being quite insistent."

"No worries."

Darrin swung open the door to find himself face to face

with what he had to admit was a spectacular pair of breasts. A spectacular pair of breasts that was covered by nothing more than a sheer white bustier.

His gaze flashed up to the breast owner's face and he barely bit back a groan at the hopeful look in the woman's eyes. Jesus, this was beyond too much.

"I'm going to have to ask you to leave."

She rested a hand on a barely covered hip and cocked her head to the side. "You know you don't mean that."

"Oh yes, I do. And if you're not off my property in the next two minutes I'm calling the cops and having you arrested for trespassing."

Matt chuckled on the other end of the line. Darrin's hand tightened on the phone. The lingerie-clad woman in front of him batted her eyelashes and pouted.

"Hey, man, let me call you back. Looks like I need to call the police," he said to Matt. Who just laughed. The asshole.

Before he could even hit the End button the woman turned and beat a hasty retreat down his front walk and to a sporty blue hatchback parked at the curb. As she flounced away Darrin couldn't help but look down—she was attractive and he was a man who generally enjoyed women—and got an eye full of bare ass. Firm, rounded bare ass.

"Apparently my unexpected visitor is familiar with squats," he said to Matt as the woman slammed her car door.

"You're seriously checking her out?"

"Dude, on the crazy-hot scale she was a solid nine."

Matt whistled. "That means she should also come with a warning label."

"Absolutely. And tell Jenn I'll be there for the wedding on Saturday." The woman sped away, waving her thong out the window as she did so. "You know what? I think I might come down a few days early."

Miranda Jacobson slowly backed away from the axis buck,

trying to figure out the best way to get his antlers untangled from the bale of hay he'd managed to get himself stuck in.

Poor little guy was caught good, and her presence only seemed to be agitating him more. Wildlife rescues could sometimes be fraught with danger, and deer were no exception with their powerful legs and sharp antlers.

Resigned, she unclipped her walkie talkie from her waistband. "Hey, Daniel, you free to help me rescue a deer?"

"Sure. What do you need and where are you?"

"I'm over by the hay bales; he got his antlers tangled in the bailing wire. Could you bring something long and sharp to cut it with?"

"No problemo. Be there in a few."

Miranda re-clipped her radio and considered the scene in front of her. Depending on what tools Daniel brought she might be able to climb on top of the bale and cut from there, which would keep her firmly out of harm's way. Otherwise, she could maybe go around to the opposite side of the bale and make the cut there. She would also have to hope like hell the buck didn't charge her or that she could get to higher ground if necessary.

A few minutes later Daniel appeared with a pole saw in one hand and a pair of loppers in the other. She raised an eyebrow but didn't say anything.

He shrugged. "What? It was the best I could come up with on short notice."

"You seriously couldn't find some wire cutters?" she muttered before saying loud enough for Daniel to hear, "Hand me the loppers."

"What? No. I'm not letting you get that close to him. He could kill you."

She rolled her eyes. "Seriously, Daniel?"

"What?"

She made a noise of frustration and took the loppers from him.

"Hey!"

"Just stay out of the way," she said as she walked towards the hay bale. There was a smaller stack of bales behind it, which she used to boost herself up onto the bigger round bale.

"What are you doing?" Daniel called.

She gritted her teeth.

"Seriously, Miranda. You're gonna get hurt."

"For the love of God, Daniel, I'm a grown ass woman and if you haven't noticed this is my freaking job. Just stop it."

His stricken expression almost made her apologize. Almost. But she'd had it up to here with his puppy dog eyes and over-protective act, especially considering she'd never given him any indication she was interested in anything other than a working friendship.

She was a single mom, for crying out loud! She barely had time to brush her hair much less think about dating.

"Sorry," Daniel mumbled.

Miranda bit back her sigh. He was a good guy—she just wasn't interested. Maybe Caridad knew someone they could set Daniel up with and focus his attention elsewhere…

The deer snorted and stomped, bringing her back to the task at hand.

What the hell was wrong with her, letting her mind wander like that with six sharp points only a few feet below her?

She collected herself and slowly inched towards the edge of the bale. First, she needed to get a better look at exactly how he was tangled before making a final game plan.

She peered over the side and was relieved to see the buck had simply managed to get one of his tines stuck in between the hay and the bailing wire. This she should be able to work with, provided the loppers would actually cut through the bailing wire.

She extended the handles as far as they would go and as slowly and quietly as possible lowered the blades towards the wire; startling the young buck could only make the situation worse. She managed to work the wire in between the blades and used every ounce of upper body strength she had to cut through the wire. The buck—still thrashing his head around—seemed momentarily confused by his sudden freedom before running away from them and the main buildings. Miranda smiled and mentally high-fived herself for a job well done.

She scrambled down from the bales and walked back over to Daniel, who had a look of scared appreciation on his face. She handed him the loppers and said, "Don't worry, I'm not gonna bite off your head again. Just have a little faith, won't ya?"

He swallowed, his Adam's apple bobbing up and down with the movement, drawing her attention to his throat. Not for the first time, it occurred to her that Daniel Hernandez was a very attractive man. Had she met him before becoming a mom and getting her heart trampled on, she probably would have been more than open to his obvious interest.

But she was a mom and she had had her heart broken by Trevor's father and, well, she didn't have time for dating or sex or even daydreaming about sex. So while Daniel's interest was flattering, it was also maddening.

"You realize you're the perfect woman, right?"

She rolled her eyes. "Whatever. I need to go check on a couple of feeders and put up a new game cam before Trevor gets home. Thanks for the loppers."

He made a sound of frustration. "Seriously, Miranda, you're absolutely perfect and I think I'm in love with you and want to marry you."

Oh, for the love of...she took a deep breath and prayed for patience. Thankfully her tone was gentle when she spoke. "Daniel, I'm flattered. I really am. And you're a great guy, but I don't have the time or the desire to be in a relationship. I'm still settling in here and I have Trevor and...I'm sorry, Daniel."

His shoulders fell and he kicked at the dirt with the toe of his boot. "I'm sorry. I shouldn't have said that just then. It was completely out of line and unprofessional."

"Hey. Don't ever apologize for expressing your feelings, okay? That way lies madness."

He looked at her and grinned. "You really are the perfect woman."

She snorted. "Hardly.

"Don't keep selling yourself short, okay?"

"I'm not. Anyway. Are we good here? I really do need to go check on those feeders before Trevor gets home from school."

"Uh, sure. Radio if you need anything."

"I will," she said as she walked towards the UTV she'd been on her way to when she'd seen the deer. She cranked the engine, shifted into Drive, and felt a huge sense of relief as she drove away from Daniel. Good Lord that had been awkward.

CHAPTER TWO

If you could meet your dream girl today, where would you want to meet her?

"WHO ARE YOU?"

Darrin looked down at the little boy who'd just walked into the house. "I'm Darrin. Who are you?"

The kid scrunched up his nose. "I'm Trevor. Did you come here to hunt?"

Darrin shook his head. "Nope. I'm here for a wedding."

A huge smile spread across Trevor's face, revealing two dimples and a missing tooth. "You know Aunt Jenn and Uncle Matt?"

Did Chase have a kid Darrin didn't know about? "Uh, yeah. Matt and I are old friends."

"Cool." Trevor opened the fridge and pulled out a juice box. "My mom says I can have one before dinner, but only one. She has a lot of rules like that."

Rules were generally a good thing when it came to kids, he'd learned. "Where is your mom?"

The boy shrugged and sipped from his juice box. "Who knows? Probably doing deer stuff."

"Deer stuff?"

"Yeah. She feeds them and stuff."

"Okay…"

"Trevor, honey, I am so sorry I wasn't here when you got home."

Darrin turned towards the new voice and felt all the air whoosh out of his body like he'd just been tackled by a three hundred pound defensive lineman. She was gorgeous, even with dust covering her jeans and what looked like dried grass stuck to the front of her shirt.

"It's okay, Mama. I was talking to Darrin."

"Darrin?" she asked as her gaze flew around the kitchen. "Oh. Hi. You must be Darrin Mann," she said as she walked into the room.

"You would be correct. And you must be Miranda." He recalled Matt mentioning that Chase and Owen had permanently hired a wildlife biologist named Miranda. They hadn't mentioned how adorable she was, though.

Adorable?

What the hell was wrong with him?

He mentally shook himself as she held out her hand in greeting. "Don't worry. I might be a mess but my hands are clean." Amusement twinkled in her brown eyes.

"That's what soap and water are for," he said, sounding like the biggest dork ever. It was as if he was still in junior high or something.

She shook his hand and quickly moved away, turning to Trevor. "Just one juice box and then it's homework time."

"I don't have any tonight."

"Where's your backpack?"

Trevor sighed heavily. "In my room."

"Why don't you go get it and let me see if you have homework?"

"Aww, Mom," he pouted.

"What have I told you about lying? Go get your homework."

Trevor set his juice box on the counter and trudged towards what Darrin assumed was his room.

Miranda turned back to him and said, "Sorry about that. He's suddenly started lying about having homework."

"Boys will be boys."

"Something like that," she muttered. "Anyway. You're here for Matt and Jenn's wedding?"

"Yes. It's still hard to believe he's getting married and going to be a dad."

"You're his agent, right?"

"Yes."

"So I'm sure you have all kinds of stories about him." She grinned.

"Not a lot that are fit for mixed company."

She drew her eyebrows together and Darrin realized how that must have sounded.

"I mean, not suitable for a woman's ears or a kid's ears."

She propped her hands on her hips. "Seriously? I work in a male-dominated field and spend ninety-five percent of my time around males—of both the two- and four-legged varieties. Believe me when I say I can handle an off-color story."

He help up his hands. "I'm sorry. I was just raised to treat women with respect."

"From what I've heard that isn't always the case."

"Excuse me?"

"Let's just say I've heard some interesting stories."

"From who?"

She shook her head. "I'm not about to reveal my sources. Now, where in the world is that boy?"

Before he could say anything else she was gone, walking in the same direction Trevor had, leaving him to wonder what kinds of stories Matt was telling about him.

Miranda took a deep breath and tried to calm her racing heart as she went in search of her son.

She'd completely forgotten about the text message Chase had sent her earlier letting her know Darrin would be staying in one of the guest rooms for the next few days or so. He was the one owner of the Devils Ranch she'd never met, and from what she'd gathered he was pretty much a silent partner.

She had not been prepared for all that intense hotness.

Sure, they were from two completely different worlds, but she still had eyes and holy fudge monkeys, Batman, Darrin Mann was hot.

She gave herself a little get-it-together shake and walked into Trevor's room.

"What are you doing?"

Trevor looked up from the Spiderman figure in his hand and blinked. "Playing super hero."

"Did you forget about bringing me your backpack?"

"Oh, yeah. Spiderman was lonely, though."

What was she going to do with this kid? "Well, you could've brought Spiderman with you."

"Yeah. I bet he would like Darrin."

Miranda highly doubted Darrin Mann gave a crap about Spiderman, but she wasn't about to tell Trevor that. "I bet he would. Let's see your homework, though, kiddo."

He grumbled but pulled a crumpled sheaf of paper from his backpack. Miranda smoothed it out and bit back a sigh.

Math.

Of course.

Trevor, for all of his imagination and precociousness, hated math.

She forced a false note of happiness into her voice. "Alright, buck-o, let's go back to the kitchen so you can work on math and finish your juice while I get supper started."

"Mo-om."

"No whining. It's gotta be done."

Trevor slowly climbed to his feet—Spiderman still clutched in his small fist—and trudged to the kitchen like a prisoner walking the plank. He might hate math, but he sure had a talent for drama.

Just like his father her dad's voice echoed in her head.

Ugh.

Trevor was nothing like his father.

Well, except there was the whole drama thing.

And his curly brown hair and bright blue eyes. And his smile and dimples and chin.

At least he'd gotten her nose.

Trevor plopped into a chair at the table set up in the breakfast nook, his juice box and Spiderman keeping watch. She grabbed a pencil and set it and his homework in front of him. "Buck-up, kiddo. You'll thank me for this one day."

And now she heard her mom's voice in her head, saying the same thing to her once upon a time.

Good Lord, she was turning into her parents.

The thought was reassuringly scary.

"But I'm gonna be a super hero, Mom. Super heroes don't need math."

"Sure they do," she said as she moved into the kitchen.

"For what? Why do you need math if you have X-Ray vision and can fly?"

She opened the fridge door and pulled out the chicken she'd set out to thaw that morning. "How will you know how fast and how far you'll need to fly without calculating it?"

"Because I'll be a super hero, and super heroes just know."

How the hell did you argue with that kind of logic?

"Well, how would you figure out how much power you have left?"

"Mo-om, it's not like a car. You just know."

Maybe she'd used, "you just do," one too many times with him.

"Okay, so do your math homework because the sooner you get it done the sooner you can become a super hero."

"Okay."

Seriously? That was all it was going to take?

Deciding not to look a gift horse in the mouth, she kept her own mouth shut and placed the chicken in a pot filled with water and set it on the stove to boil before opening the refrigerator and grabbing a couple of cans of biscuits and a gallon of milk. As the chicken boiled she combined flour, salt, pepper, and onion powder into a bowl, then popped open the first can of biscuits.

"Ooh. Are we having chicken and dumplings?" Trevor asked from the table.

"Yes, sir."

She smiled as she cut each biscuit into quarters before dropping the pieces into the flour mixture. There were times when she wondered if she was cheating by using biscuits rather than making the dumplings from scratch, but this way was the way her grandmother had taught her so that's what she stuck to.

She just wished she'd been able to get Nana's secret recipe before she'd passed away a few years ago. At this point she was basically forced to recreate the dish from memory, and hers was somehow never quite right.

Miranda checked the chicken, saw it was cooking nicely, and opened the second can of biscuits. As she settled into the rhythm of making dinner, her mind wandered back to the conversation she'd had with Daniel just a few hours ago.

You're the perfect woman.

As if.

So perfect she'd gotten knocked up her senior year of college by the boy she'd dated since high school—who'd decided to join the army the day after she told him she was pregnant. She'd been crushed—and panicked—wondering what the hell she was going to do as a single mom who was slated to start grad school in just a few short months.

She'd written him numerous times during her pregnancy. Each letter was met with silence. When she had Trevor his father's parents were there, as were her own. But no Joshua. Not so much as a phone call or email, despite the fact that both she and his parents had tried to reach him numerous times.

Two months after Trevor was born a man had shown up on the Blake's doorstep, informing them their son had been killed in the line of duty somewhere in Afghanistan.

Eva and Alan had been absolutely devastated to have lost their only child, and Miranda had been devastated that she'd never know if Joshua had even received her letters much less cared.

Since then, she'd hardened her heart against the allure of good-looking men—that was one road she simply wasn't willing to go down again. She'd managed to put herself through grad school and get her master's degree in wildlife biology— thanks to the help of her parents and the Blake's.

And now here she was, eight years later, making chicken and dumplings in one of the most beautiful kitchens she'd ever seen and living at one of the most exclusive hunting ranches in the state of Texas.

The sound of water boiling over and hitting open flame jolted her out of her thoughts and had her racing to turn down the heat on the chicken.

Perfect?

Ha!

She couldn't even boil chicken without messing it up.

CHAPTER THREE

*Do you believe in traditional relationship roles, or are you
more modern?*

DARRIN ENDED THE CALL WITH ONE OF HIS CLIENTS AND STEPPED
out of his room.

Something smelled good.

He followed his nose to the kitchen where Miranda was
stirring something on the stove and Trevor was sitting at the
table, a look of fierce concentration on his face.

Guess he really did have homework after all.

"Need help with anything?" he asked.

Miranda jumped, causing the spoon to fly out of her hand.
She spun around with a hand over heart. "Good Lord, you
scared me."

He fought a smile at the sight of her still dirty but now also
covered in flour self. "I'm sorry."

She turned back to the stove and grabbed the spoon that
had flown out of her hand. "No worries. I wasn't sure what
your dinner plans were so I made more than enough for everyone. Hope you like chicken and dumplings, otherwise it's
a little far to go for takeout."

"I haven't had chicken and dumplings since I was a kid. It
sounds perfect."

She turned her head and flicked her gaze over him. "Yeah, you don't exactly strike me as the down home cookin' type."

"What's that supposed to mean?"

She chuckled. "Forgive me, Mr. Mann, but I'm pretty sure your jeans cost more than my entire wardrobe and your hands are in better shape than mine will ever be."

He moved until he stood next to the counter a few feet away from her. "First, you can call me Darrin. Second, that was a lot of assuming you just did."

"Was I wrong, though?"

He let out a sigh. "No, you weren't wrong."

She pointed the spoon in his direction. "Ha! Of course I wasn't. And I'm not saying wearing expensive jeans or getting a manicure is a bad thing. I'm just guessing you're much more used to eating prime rib or foie gras at five star restaurants than you are chicken and dumplin's at a ranch in the middle of nowhere."

"No to the foie gras. Yes to everything else. And the highest rating a restaurant can get is three stars according to Michelin."

"Michelin as in the tire company?"

He held up his hands. "Beats me, I don't understand it, either. But it's the most respected restaurant rating system out there."

She looked at him askance before turning the heat off on the stove and moving to the refrigerator where she removed a bowl filled with salad. She set it on the counter then took out a few bottles of different kinds of dressings and a pitcher of what looked like tea, which she also set on the counter.

"Okay, kiddo. Time to set aside the homework and go wash your hands for dinner."

"Yes!" Trevor pumped his fist in the air as he scrambled out of his chair.

"Boring homework, I take it?"

"Math," she said as she set bowls and plates on the counter.

"In that case, I completely understand where he's coming from."

"Not a fan of mathematics, I take it?"

"More that math and I just don't get along." He wasn't about to go into the details of why—his dyscalculia was a weakness he never discussed with anyone.

"I think it's the same for Trevor. He's great with words and loves to read, but math is a struggle."

Trevor came scrambling back into the kitchen, a Spiderman figure clutched in one hand. "Mom, Spidey wants some chicken and dumplings, too."

Darrin bit back a chuckle.

"Uh, no. I think Spidey will be just fine. Why don't you go set out the silverware and napkins?"

"Fine." Trevor's bottom lip stuck out in the briefest pout Darrin had ever seen. His nieces and nephews could learn a thing or two from this kid.

"What do you need me to do?" he asked.

"Um, I guess you can plate the salad if you want to."

He picked up the salad tongs that were on the counter and busied himself serving salad while Miranda ladled chicken and dumplings into bowls.

They took their places at the table and before he could pick up his fork, Miranda and Trevor had bowed their heads in prayer.

Something he only seemed to do these days at family gatherings during the holidays.

"Dear Lord, thank you for my mom and this awesome food. Amen."

Darrin barely managed not to snicker at the little boy's ability to cut right to the chase. There was definitely something to be said about simplicity, though.

He looked up to find Miranda's lips twitching in a barely repressed grin, and the sight did some weird twisty thing in his gut that he hadn't felt...maybe ever.

Talk about inconvenient.

He pushed all thoughts and feelings of attraction out of the way and focused on the meal in front of him. It was much simpler than what he'd grown accustomed to, which made him feel a little like a spoiled brat considering once upon a time meals like this had been considered gourmet in his world.

"How was school today?" Miranda asked Trevor.

He swallowed before saying, "Okay."

"Just okay?"

He shrugged. "Yeah."

"Still having trouble making friends?"

"I miss Alison."

"Honey, you're too young for a girlfriend."

Darrin somehow managed to not laugh. Oh, to be a kid again.

"She wasn't my girlfriend, Mom. She was my best friend. And I miss her."

"Oh, sweetie, you'll make new friends. I promise."

Darrin smiled at Miranda. "New school?"

"Yeah. Before Chase and Owen offered me this position— and the option to live on the property—we lived in town in Del Rio. Out here the school district is Comstock, which is much smaller than what Trevor's used to. It'll just take time."

"I'll admit I know nothing about this area, other than it's in the middle of nowhere and close to Mexico."

She snorted. "How is that possible? Aren't you one of the owners?"

"Kind of a silent owner. Long story short, Matt approached me with the opportunity to invest in some land and I figured it would be a smart decision considering they're not exactly making any more of it."

"You have a valid point."

"I thought so." He paused and took another bite of his dinner. "This is really good, by the way."

"Thanks."

"Anyway. I travel a lot for my job and at certain times of the year it seems like I'm rarely home. When I am I'm in meetings or on a call, which isn't exactly conducive to getting away to the middle of nowhere."

"Are you a superhero?" Trevor asked.

"Nope. Not even close."

"What do you do?" he asked.

"I'm a sports agent."

Trevor crinkled his nose. "What's a sports agent?"

How to explain this to a kid who looked to be around eight years old? "Who's your favorite athlete?"

"Uncle Matt!"

Darrin grinned. "Good choice. So when Matt was playing baseball, his job was with the Wranglers and he got paid a lot of money to throw a baseball. I'm his agent, so I helped him negotiate for that money."

"Oh. That doesn't sound like fun."

"It can be fun, especially when I get to go to football, basketball, and baseball games. And I get to meet some really cool people."

"Like who?"

"Well, there's Matt for starters. And Caridad—you know her, right?"

Trevor nodded. "Yup. That's Uncle Owen's girlfriend. She's nice."

Nice wasn't a word he'd ever considered associating with Caridad Mathews considering she could be a bit of a ball-buster, but if the kid thought she was nice, more power to him.

"I met Caridad because of my job—she needed someone to negotiate some advertising stuff for her—and she and I became friends." He named off a few other athletes he figured Trevor had heard of, making the kid's face light up with each one.

"Cool!" He turned to Miranda. "Mom, I wanna be a sports agent when I grow up."

Her expression was thankfully amused rather than angry at Trevor's latest declaration. "If that's what you want to do, I'm all for it, kiddo."

"Sweet!"

Darrin shook his head and dove back into his supper, thinking this was the most relaxed he'd been in a long time.

Miranda shut Trevor's bedroom door behind her and leaned against it, her eyes closed and her body almost melting into the wood. Bedtime was always a chore with Trevor, mostly because he wanted to stay up and read and she knew that if he did that he wouldn't fall asleep until two in the freaking morning. And then he would be cranky when she had to wake him up a few hours later for school.

She guessed her son being a bookworm was a good problem to have on her hands.

She exhaled slowly and pushed away from the door, heading towards the living room for her nightly catch-up with the world, which mostly consisted of mindlessly playing around on Facebook until she could barely keep her eyes open. Sometimes she went a little crazy and turned on the news in the background.

She was officially the most boring thirty year-old ever.

The sight of Darrin sitting on the couch, an open laptop on his lap and reading glasses perched on the end of his nose almost caused her to trip over her own feet.

Attractiveness, a great job, and now reading glasses? So not fair.

He looked up and smiled at her as she walked into the room. "I'm not disturbing you, am I?"

Not unless you take into consideration all of your hotness, nope, not at all.

"You have just as much of a right to be here as I do," she said instead, and almost instantly regretted the tone of her words. She'd sounded kind of bitchy.

"You live here, though, and have a routine. I'm disrupting that."

She grabbed her tablet then sat down in one of the huge,

overstuffed arm chairs. "As long as you don't mind me vegging out while watching Lip Sync Battle snippets on YouTube, you're not disrupting anything."

Yeah, she sometimes did that, too.

She led such an exciting life.

"I love that show. Veg away."

"You like something as plebeian as Lip Sync Battle?"

"Do I come across as that much of a snob?"

She shrugged, hoping the gesture looked casual. "Kind of."

"How? If I may ask?"

She thought longingly of LL Cool J and wished she'd never said anything. "Well, like I mentioned earlier, your clothes are kind of a dead giveaway. And there's just something about the way you carry yourself that makes it obvious you're not on the same level as us mere mortal folk who are happy to be able to sock away a few dollars every month for an emergency savings fund."

His eyebrows drew together over those green eyes that were startling against his light brown skin. "Are we not paying you enough?"

Her cheeks warmed. "That's not what I meant at all. Y'all are actually paying me really well, and living here is definitely a financial help. I was just speaking in general terms. Y'know, for the entire middle class. Which I probably shouldn't have done. And I'm going to shut up now."

Before he could say anything else she popped a pair of ear buds into her ears and pulled up the black hole that was YouTube. Screw Facebook, now that she'd mentioned Lip Sync Battle she was totally re-watching some previous clips.

God knew she could use the laughs, and Anne Hathaway's rendition of "Wrecking Ball" was sure to get the job done.

Some time later she was jolted awake by a warm hand on her shoulder. She sat up and pulled her ear buds out of her ears and blinked a few times to clear the fog. The most attractive man she'd seen in a long time—which was saying something, considering her bosses were all grade-A hotties and Daniel honestly wasn't too bad himself—stood beside her, a grin twisting his full, sensuous lips and laughter sparkling in his green eyes.

Best. Dream. Ever.

When she felt another small shake of her shoulder, Miranda opened her eyes again and shook her head, and promptly realized she hadn't been dreaming.

There really was a super hot man standing right beside her.

"Did you know you snore when you sleep?" Darrin teased.

She felt her cheeks get warm. "No, I don't."

"Yes, you do. I heard you. Don't worry, though, you're a quiet snorer. It's kind of cute."

Cute. Just what every woman wanted to be called.

Although considering she'd apparently been snoring, cute probably wasn't a bad thing.

"Sorry if I disturbed you."

"Not at all. I figured you'd probably want to get up and go to bed, though, rather than getting a crick in your neck by sleeping in the chair all night."

She instinctively rolled her head on said neck. "Thanks. Good night."

She scrambled up from the chair, taking her tablet and all of her awkwardness with her.

Darrin heard a shower come on a few minutes later and bit back a groan.

This attraction to Miranda was so unfortunate.

One, she was kind of his employee.

Two, he was only going to be here for a few days and would go back to Dallas as soon as Matt and Jenn tied the knot.

Three, she was a single mom, and one of his hard and fast rules was no single moms. Not that he didn't like kids, but that was a lot of baggage. Not to mention a lot of juggling. Considering his job kept him juggling enough as it was, he didn't need to add somebody else's kid on top of that.

Four, she was kind of prickly and didn't seem to think too highly of him.

And five...hell. He forgot what his fifth reason was. The first four would have to suffice.

His phone dinged with an incoming text message as he sat back down on the couch.

Matt: You made it to the ranch okay, right?

Darrin: It's almost midnight and you're just now thinking to ask me that?

Matt: Fuck off smart ass. We'll all be out there tomorrow, so get ready.

Darrin: I was born ready.

Matt: You're kind of lame. Why are you my best friend again?

Darrin: Because I helped negotiate the largest contract ever for a pitcher over age 30?

Matt: Oh, yeah. There was that little thing.

Darrin: Teeny tiny.

Matt: That's what she said.

Darrin: You've reverted to high school.

Matt: According to Jenn I've never left.

Darrin: She's probably right.

Matt: Yup. See you in the morning, bro.

Darrin chuckled as he re-pocketed his phone. It would be good to see Matt again, considering he'd only seen him a couple of times since he'd pitched a perfect Game Seven of the World Series and subsequently retired. Matt had been one of his first clients, and they'd instantly become friends.

He was still adjusting to no longer negotiating advertising deals and baseball contracts for him, but he was also really happy his best friend had found love and was perfectly content to settle down with a wife and a kid.

Sometimes he kind of envied him.

Darrin pinched the bridge of his nose and gathered up his laptop and reading glasses. Being around Trevor even for a few hours today had made him realize how much he missed his nieces and nephews—eight of them, last time he'd counted—and he made a mental note to take the time to go down to Beaumont to see them.

The shower turned off as he was walking into the bedroom he'd been led toward earlier that afternoon, and he forced himself not to think about what Miranda might look like naked.

This was going to be a long few days.

CHAPTER FOUR

How would your friends describe you?

"DUDE, HOW THE HELL HAVE YOU BEEN?" MATT ASKED BEFORE pulling Darrin in for a hug.

He laughed and said, "You know me. Busy making other people money."

"And fighting off women from what I hear," Matt's soon to be wife Jenn said, grinning at him.

Darrin hugged her and said, "Yeah, that's gotten a little ridiculous."

A pickup he recognized all too well pulled up just then, and the truck had barely stopped before the driver's side door was open and Caridad was heading towards him. He wrapped his arms around her and picked her up in a bear hug before setting her back on the ground and looking down at her. "Holy shit. I think love might be good for you."

She punched him in the arm.

"Cari, are you sure you want to punch the man who's negotiating a TV contract for you?" her boyfriend, and one of the other ranch owners, Owen asked.

"Eh, he'll get a nice little cut of it. Besides, he knows that punching him is the least amount of damage I could do."

Truth. Caridad happened to be the reigning Women's Three-Gun Champion and was competing at a level so far this season that was blowing away what she'd done the previous year. Considering how rough she'd had it for so long, he couldn't think of anyone who deserved the success—and the happiness—she was now experiencing more.

A big black truck pulled up beside Caridad's and came to a stop. Moments later Matt's younger brother, Chase, Chase's wife Jo, and the largest dog Darrin had ever seen got out and walked towards them. Well, the dog ran off, sniffing at everything in sight and then peeing on it. Even though he hadn't seen Chase since the World Series at the beginning of October, it was obvious even to him that the other man had lost a decent amount of weight since then, making his once lean and muscular frame look long and ropey.

"Long time, no see," he said as he shook Chase's hand.

"Glad you could make it. Someone needs to make sure Matt has a tight leash on him."

"Hey!" Jenn exclaimed.

"Not that kind of leash, babe," Matt stage whispered, making Jenn blush to the roots of her curly auburn hair.

"Oh, shut up you big perv."

One thing Darrin really liked about Jenn—she gave Matt as good as she got. That took talent and a lot of backbone.

"Anyone need help carrying in anything?" he asked.

"Sure," Jenn said, and he followed her and Matt to Matt's JEEP.

"Jesus. How much clothing did you need?" he teased.

"Shut it. I'm seven months pregnant and getting married in a few days. I wanted to make sure I had everything I needed just in case."

"Just in case what?"

Jenn shrugged. "In case I needed it."

"Her parents are preppers," Matt said by way of explanation.

"They're what?"

"Preppers. Like on that TV show?" Matt said.

"No clue."

Jenn sighed. "I guess I know what we'll all be watching on Netflix later."

Matt chuckled and kissed the top her head. "We don't have to if you don't want to."

"It's okay. Hell, I probably need to brush up on the show so I can be prepared when my parents' episode comes on."

Darrin dragged two suitcases behind him as they headed towards the house. "Your parents' episode?"

"Yeah. Unfortunately they were asked to be featured on Doomsday Preppers, which is the show we're talking about. They apparently wrapped up filming about a month ago, so who knows when the episode will actually air."

"I take it you're not happy about this?"

"Would you be happy if your parents were weirdo preppers who lived in retrofitted storage containers in the middle of nowhere and thought a good science project was making your little sister stir shit in the composting toilet?"

Darrin almost choked on air. "Excuse me?"

"Exactly. They're effing crazy. Crazy I tell you."

Darrin met Matt's gaze and saw the other man was trying not to laugh, which made his own laughter harder to hold back.

"Look at it this way, babe, if it hadn't been for all of those condoms your mom sent you that day you and I might not have ever gotten together."

Jenn snorted. "Oh, whatever. You and I both know we would have gotten together anyway."

Matt grinned as they walked into the living room. "Yeah, we would have. I was already wearing you down pretty good."

Jenn flipped him the bird as she walked ahead of them towards the bedrooms.

"That's not very ladylike."

"Screw ladylike."

"God, I love that woman."

Darrin did laugh then, a deep chuckle that shook his chest and had his belly aching. "She's pretty much perfect for you, man."

"No kidding. I don't think anyone else would have been able to put up with my shit."

"She's certainly brave."

Matt's gaze softened briefly, so filled with love it almost made Darrin's teeth ache. "That she is."

As they made their way down the hall, Darrin clenched his jaw and steeled his spine. He had a good life in Dallas.

Crazy, scantily-clad women aside.

"Uncle Matt! Aunt Jenn!" Trevor yelled as he ran into the house ahead of Miranda.

"Inside voice, young man!" she chided as her son ran towards Matt and crashed into his legs. Matt picked Trevor up and swung him above his head, making him laugh and Miranda smile.

When Matt had first started spending more time at the ranch and thus around them, they'd both been a little in awe of the former all-star pitcher. Matt, though, had worked to put them both at ease and had taken Trevor under his wing, for which Miranda would be eternally grateful.

Trevor's father might not have ever been around, but he was a lucky little boy to have Chase, Matt, Owen, and even Daniel in his life on a regular basis.

Matt set Trevor down, who immediately ran to Jenn. He somehow managed to slow himself just in time, and his hug with her was much gentler.

"Hey there, little man. How was school?"

Trevor pulled a face at the former seventh grade teacher. "It was okay."

"Just okay?"

He shrugged. "Yeah. I guess."

Jenn and Miranda's eyes met across the room, and Miranda shrugged before saying, "Trevor, honey, why don't you go put your backpack in your room and go outside and play for a while?"

"But I wanna see Aunt Jenn and Uncle Matt."

"We'll be here the next few days, little man, so why don't you go outside and play for a while?" Jenn said as she ruffled his hair.

"Okay," he pouted as he walked off.

"I swear, that kid can pull a guilt trip like you wouldn't believe," Miranda said as she walked over to Jenn and gave her a hug.

"He's adorable, though, so he can totally get away with it. Besides, he's the future husband of my to-be born daughter, so you better believe I'm going to be sweet to him."

Miranda laughed and Matt said, "Babe, we are not marrying our daughter off before she's even born, especially considering she won't be allowed to date until she's at least thirty."

"He's already got the overprotective daddy thing down pat," Jenn said.

"Obviously," Miranda agreed.

Trevor ran out of his bedroom and out the front door, slamming it behind him. Miranda sighed and shook her head.

"Is he still having trouble adjusting to the new school?" Jenn asked.

"Yeah. He misses his friends, which I totally understand. And he's out here all by himself most days which probably isn't incredibly fun."

"I would imagine not, but he'll adjust. It'll just take some time."

"I'm guessing there aren't any other kids nearby?" Matt asked.

"A handful, but you know how far apart everything is out here. It's not the same as living in town and just going next door, y'know."

"I'm sure if you wanted to move back into Del Rio the boys would be fine with that," Jenn said.

"Of course we would."

Jenn rolled her eyes at Matt. "You're not the one who

hired her."

"So? I'm still part owner and the big brother."

Just then Jo walked in from down the hall, a worried expression on her face.

"He's not feeling well, is he?" Jenn asked.

Jo shook her head and blew out a breath. "No, not really. It seems like he's having more bad days than good here lately. It's looking like he's barely going to make it to the transplant without having to go on dialysis."

Chase—Jo's husband, Matt's younger brother, and one of Miranda's main bosses—had found out late last year that he was going into kidney failure and would need either a transplant or dialysis to survive. Over the past few months Miranda had seen him out at the ranch less and less, and when she had he'd been noticeably thinner with a yellowish cast to his once-tanned skin.

Matt and Jenn shared a look—one of those secretive looks every couple seemed to end up sharing at some point in their relationship—and Miranda felt a brief pang of jealousy. Most days she was fine just doing her thing and being Trevor's mom. Some days, though, she really longed for things she no longer had.

"When is the transplant?" Miranda asked, bringing her thoughts back to the topic at hand.

"Two weeks from now," Matt said.

"Wow. So, soon."

"Yes, thank God," he said, a grim look on his face.

Miranda pulled out a chair and sat down, making herself comfortable. "So how'd that come about anyway? I mean, what's the process for being a living donor?"

Matt shrugged. "It wasn't too bad, really. As soon as we found out living donors could start applying online I did it, along with a bunch of other people. I don't know how many made it past the initial online screening to get blood work done, but I know both Owen and I did. They moved me through the process first since we're brothers, and basically I just had to get a bunch of labs done, an EKG, an ultrasound, talk to a social worker, stuff like that. We didn't find out until a couple of weeks ago that we'd both been approved by the board, and two weeks from now was the best time for everyone involved scheduling wise."

"Where's the surgery taking place?"

"At Baylor up in Dallas," Jo said.

"Why not in San Antonio? It's closer," Miranda asked.

"For a number of reasons. One, his nephrologist actually recommended Baylor over everyone else in the state because they have a fantastic kidney transplant program that's been highly successful. Two," Jo said, holding up a second finger, "Matt has a house in Dallas that we can all stay at post-op, which is a blessing considering Chase and I are going to be there for at least four to six weeks post-transplant and Matt will need to be there for a week post-surgery."

"Makes sense. Why do you have to stay there so long after the transplant?"

"Checkups. For the first couple of weeks he'll have to go to the transplant institute three times a week for checkups to make sure his medication levels are normal, to make sure his labs look good, he's healing well, stuff like that from what I understand. Right now it all feels incredibly overwhelming, and even having done a crap ton of research I still feel completely unprepared for this."

"I would imagine most people in your shoes would feel that way, hon," Jenn said with a sympathetic smile on her face.

"Probably. That seems to be the consensus on the caretaker support forums, at least."

"Wait," Miranda said, "you're a high school counselor and yet you're checking out online support forums?"

Jo shrugged. "It's actually a decent form of research. People tend to be very honest when they're speaking anonymously. And we've gone to a few therapy sessions together, just to talk it out with someone else. It's a lot to deal with considering, y'know, life and death here."

Miranda snorted. "No kidding. I can't even imagine what you must be going through. Or you, either," she said, turning to Jenn. "I mean, you're getting married in a couple of days, you're pregnant, and your husband's about to donate a kidney to his brother. That's kind of a big deal."

Jenn waved it off. "I'm fine. I'll just be glad to know Chase is healthy again. Matt's already proven that he's a stubborn bastard who heals unusually fast, so I'm not too worried about that."

Considering Matt had taken a line drive to the head less than a year ago that had left him with a cracked skull and a brain bleed, it was amazing he was whole and healthy today, much less the fact that he'd actually returned to the majors last season and pitched lights out in the World Series before retiring.

"And look at it this way, Chase is almost as stubborn as I am, so once he has one of my kidneys he'll just be extra stubborn with a dose of awesome."

Jenn rolled her eyes at her future husband. "He's definitely not lacking in self-esteem."

"And you know you love it."

"I do?" Jenn asked, making everyone laugh.

"Where's Owen and Caridad? I noticed her truck out front but haven't seen them yet."

"I do believe she wanted to get in some range time since she leaves on Sunday for a match," Jenn said.

"Which means Owen's probably with her and they're probably having sex in the middle of hot brass," Matt said.

"Okay, that's just weird," Miranda said. "And I did not need that mental image."

"He's probably being facetious," Jenn said.

"Or I could be right on the money. You know how those two are. She's all about guns, ammo, and Owen and he's all about Caridad and guns. It's pretty much a match made in heaven."

"Seriously, that's more than I need to know about my

boss."

Jo nudged Miranda with the toe of her shoe. "You and Caridad have become pretty good friends, haven't you?"

She shrugged. "Yeah, I guess so. I mean, neither of us are the girly girl type and both of us work in a very male-dominated industry, so we've kind of bonded over that. Why?"

"Just curious. She's a tough cookie to crack."

"She is," Miranda hedged, "but she has her reasons, which I'm pretty sure all of you probably know by now."

Jenn, Jo, and Matt all nodded at Miranda's veiled reference to the abusive ex-boyfriend Caridad had dealt with and ultimately had to defend her life from just before Christmas.

"It's been a really crazy past year," Jo chuckled.

"No kidding," Jenn said. "First you come back last summer and fall in love with Chase. Matt gets hit in the head and somehow makes me fall in love with him and knocks me up in the process. Then there was the World Series. Caridad came to town and Owen fell head over heels in love with her. Chase found out he needed a transplant and like two weeks later y'all got married. Caridad shot her ex-boyfriend that same night. Darrin was just declared Dallas' Most Eligible Bachelor, and now here we are two days before my wedding and two weeks before Chase's kidney transplant. I think I covered everything, right?"

"I think those were the high notes, at least," Jo said.

"Wow. Never have I been so thankful for my super boring life. The most exciting thing that's happened to me recently is having to free a deer from a hay bale and Daniel asking me to marry him."

Jenn did a double take. "What? Daniel asked you to marry him? But you're not even dating! Or sleeping together. Right?"

Miranda laughed. "Right. None of the above. And I think it was more a joke than anything else, but I had to put him in his place which wasn't all that fun. So if he's sulky the next few days, that's why."

"So this was recent?"

"As in, yesterday."

"Ah."

"Yeah."

"If you need me to take care of him and have a little chat with him, let me know," Matt said.

"I don't think that'll be necessary, but thank you. He's a good guy who's unfortunately developed a bit of a crush, I think. He just needs to meet someone else and he'll forget about me just like that," she said, snapping her fingers.

"I don't think you're giving yourself enough credit," Jenn said.

Miranda shrugged. "It's not a matter of credit, really, more just simple honesty. Anyway. Enough about that. It's water under the bridge. Speaking of where are people, where's Darrin? I figured he'd be spending all the time he could with y'all while he's here."

"He had some calls to make. Spring training's almost over and he has a couple of last minute contract things to take care of."

"He's quite attractive, isn't he?" Jenn asked, her green eyes sparkling.

Miranda giggle snorted. "You could definitely say that."

"Come on, that's my best friend and agent you're talking about!"

"So?" Jenn asked innocently.

"Fair enough. Even I have to admit the guy was labeled Dallas' Most Eligible Bachelor for a reason."

"He hasn't said a word about that since he got here yesterday, by the way."

"I would imagine not. What he thought could be a great PR move has ended up backfiring on him a little bit."

Jenn leaned towards Miranda and stage whispered, "A naked woman showed up at his house the other night."

"Woah. That's crazy."

"I know, right? But from what I understand, that's par for

the course for some of these guys."

Miranda glanced at Matt, who put up his hands and said, "Not me anymore."

"Anymore," Jo teased.

"Hey, you stay out of it. It's not like your husband hasn't had his fair share of random naked chicks, too."

"I am so glad they stopped showing up before I came back to town. Because, seriously, I will throat punch somebody."

Everyone laughed, but Miranda had a sneaking suspicion Jo wasn't entirely kidding—the woman was pretty good with a pistol and seemed to be willing to do just about anything for her husband.

Including throat punch a random naked woman, apparently.

CHAPTER FIVE

How would you describe your sense of humor?

"I FIGURED I'D FIND YOU GUYS OUT HERE," DARRIN SAID AS HE closed the door to the range behind him.

Owen and Caridad turned from the table they were set up at, Caridad smiling as he drew closer.

"Where else would I be? I have a big match coming up next week I need to practice for. What's up?"

"I heard back from Outdoor TV last night and they sent over the final copies of the contract this morning. Looks like your show's a go."

She turned and looked at Owen, who wore an expression of pride on his face.

"I can't believe I'm going to have my own TV show."

"You deserve it, and then some, Cari," Owen said.

"You're just saying that because you love me."

"Well, that, too."

She elbowed him before turning back to Darrin. "So do we know anything yet about production schedules or anything?"

"Not yet. This basically means the contract's been negotiated, we know what you're going to be compensated and how many initial episodes are being requested. Scheduling talk should begin within the next couple of weeks, I would think."

Caridad took a series of deep, even breaths and closed her

eyes.

"You okay?" Owen murmured.

She nodded her head. "Just trying not to hyperventilate."

Owen rubbed her back. "Just breathe, Cari. You're gonna be fine."

"I know. I know. It's just a lot to take in." She drew in a shaky breath. "Hot damn it's been a crazy past six months."

Considering she'd lost her grandmother, won the national women's Three Gun title, broken up with her former boyfriend, moved from Dallas back home to Del Rio, met and fallen in love with Owen, and had a frightening experience with her abusive high school sweetheart...Darrin would say the past six months had been beyond crazy for Caridad.

"I'm not sure 'crazy' is the word I would use, I just can't think of anything more appropriate."

"One hot mess of a clusterfuck?" she asked.

"I think that probably covers it," Owen said. "Anyway, glad you finally got a chance to make it down here, considering your name's on the deed and all."

Darrin laughed. "Yeah, I know. I rarely get the chance to get away for even a few hours, much less a few days. Negotiations are pretty much twenty-four seven."

"Well, I'm glad you finally did what I've been telling you for years you needed to do and took a vacation, even if it's only for a few days," Caridad said.

"I honestly probably wouldn't have if a mostly naked woman hadn't shown up on my doorstep the night before last."

Owen raised a red eyebrow. "You're complaining about a naked woman showing up on your doorstep?"

"She was at least a nine on the crazy/hot scale."

"Yeah, I would have run away from that, too."

"Anyway. I didn't mean to disturb you two. Caridad, I'll let you get back to your practice; you have matches to win and a title to defend."

"You don't have to go. I love getting to spend some time

with you."

Darrin waved her words away. "We'll have plenty of time over the next couple of days. I have more calls I need to make anyway, and it's looking like one of my guys might get to start the season in the majors this year rather than the minors, and negotiating that is priority right now."

"I guess we'll catch up later, then," Caridad smiled and turned back to the shooting bench, effectively dismissing him. Darrin smiled and shook his head, and Owen just shrugged before putting his ear plugs back in and turning back to his girlfriend.

Darrin opened the door and walked back outside, his mind torn between the call he had in fifteen minutes with the Wranglers regarding their rookie outfielder, and the palpable affection between Owen and Caridad. Never in a million years would he have thought to see Caridad so happy and at ease. The guarded look was gone from her eyes, and while she would never be what anyone would describe as "bubbly," she was certainly more relaxed than he'd ever seen her.

For that alone he would have liked Owen.

His phone vibrating in his pocket interrupted his thoughts, and he pulled it out to find a text message from his assistant, Samantha.

Samantha: A delivery guy just showed up with two dozen roses.

Darrin: Okay…

Samantha: They're not for me. They're for you.

Darrin: What?

Samantha: They're for you. I'm sending you some pics so you can see how obnoxious they are.

Seconds later his phone vibrated with two incoming photos. The first was of a bouquet that was, yes, obnoxious. Who sent a man two dozen pink roses anyway? The second was of the card, which he zoomed in on so he could read it.

Darrin,

Thanks for last night. It was fabulous.

Love,

Maddie

Samantha: I thought you were in the middle of nowhere?

Darrin: I am.

Samantha: Then who's Maddie?

If Samantha wasn't such an amazing executive assistant he would seriously consider talking to her about overstepping her boundaries. But the fact was, she was the best EA he'd ever had and was one of the few people in his life who wasn't afraid to give him hell.

It honestly made him respect her more.

Darrin: I have no idea. I don't know anyone named Maddie.

Samantha: Whoever she is, she has awful taste in flowers.

Darrin: No kidding.

Samantha: I wonder if Steve would give me a cut of his profits.

He chuckled at the reference to the man who sold roses from a bucket day in and day out from the street corner below their office. Steve was incredibly nice, and a favorite of everyone in the building thanks to his booming laugh and constant smile.

Darrin: I doubt it. He's pretty stingy with his money.

Samantha: Oh, well, a girl can hope. Anyway. I'll get rid of them…unless you want me to keep them?

Darrin: God, no. I don't care what you do with them.

Samantha: Noted. Anyway. I'm about to head out. Just thought you'd want to know about the flowers.

Darrin: Have a good evening. Thanks for taking care of them.

Samantha: No problem.

Darrin re-pocketed his phone and sighed. Maddie? Who the hell was Madd—oh, hell.

He walked into the house and found Matt, Jenn, Jo, and Miranda all sitting at the dining room table chatting. Matt looked up and almost immediately started laughing.

The asshole.

"Nice flowers, Maddie. Now you have my assistant thinking I'm having random hookups in the middle of nowhere."

Matt nearly doubled over laughing, and Jenn just stared at her future husband in confusion.

"Okay, what am I missing here?"

"Your groom apparently thought it would be funny to send these to me at my office today," Darrin said, handing his phone—with the photos pulled up—to Jenn.

Who also burst into laughter.

"Dear God, Matt, those are awful." Jenn turned the phone so Matt could see the roses.

"I know," Matt said in between laughs. He took a few deep breaths. "I told the girl at the flower shop to send the most atrociously feminine pink roses they had. She really outdid herself. I think I need to call back tomorrow and give her an additional tip."

Jenn handed him back his phone, and Darrin took it while fighting back a smile. "Jenn, are you sure you want to marry this guy? He has the sense of humor of a fourteen-year-old."

"Well, considering how he kinda sorta knocked me up… yeah."

With a lot of other couples, a statement like that would make one wonder if the wedding was happening simply to give the baby legitimacy. In the case of Matt and Jenn, though, it was obvious that Jenn was joking; they were absolutely head over heels for each other, and the baby was just a happy bonus for them both as far as they were concerned.

His phone vibrated again, and he looked at the screen before saying, "Sorry, guys, I have to take this. Later."

He hit accept as he walked back towards the bedroom that had become his temporary office, prepared to go to bat for his client and determined to put any feelings of unease behind him.

CHAPTER SIX

How do you like to spend your free time?

THEY MADE HOMEMADE PIZZAS THAT NIGHT FOR SUPPER, THE living area of the ranch house full of laughter, good-natured teasing, and friendship. Trevor thoroughly enjoyed being the center of attention—not to mention Winchester's constant presence at his side.

Putting him to bed that night was an even more epic struggle than usual, and he only relented when she gave in and told him the Great Pyrenees could indeed sleep in his room. Once her boy—and Chase's boy—had finally settled down for the night, Miranda pulled his bedroom door shut and walked outside to join everyone else around the fire pit.

"Finally get him to go to bed?" Caridad asked as she sat down beside her.

Miranda blew out a heavy sigh. "Finally. I basically had to bribe him with Winchester." She looked across the fire at Chase. "Sorry, boss, but I think your dog's adopted my son."

Chase laughed. "Win loves kids. There's a boy a couple of houses down who plays basketball in his driveway all the time, and Win will just sit there, staring out the window whining."

"Aww. He needs a little brother or sister," Jenn said, the corner of her mouth quirking upwards.

"That is so not happening right now," Jo said.

Jenn patted her best friend's knee and said, "I know. I was talking about a puppy. But even then, now isn't a good time, all things considered."

Jo's smile was kind of sad as her gaze slid to her husband. "Yeah, definitely not right now. Maybe post-transplant, we'll think about it."

Miranda's heart twisted just a little for Chase and Jo. She didn't know much about their story, but she knew enough and that they'd been best friends as children, drifted apart, and met again last summer when they fell in love. It almost seemed unfair for two newlyweds to be dealing with such serious issues as literal life and death, but from what she could tell they were handling it splendidly.

"At any rate, he'll have a niece in a few months, which I'm sure he'll love," Jenn said.

Chase snorted. "Will Matt even let my dog around her?"

"Maybe," Matt said, "as long as he swears to protect her and not let any boys get within twenty feet of her."

"With the exception of Trevor, since he's our future son-in-law, honey," Jenn teased.

Matt shook his head. "Nope. Not thinking about it. She's never dating or having sex or getting married."

"He's really got this protective dad thing down pat already," Miranda whispered to Caridad.

"No kidding. And the crazy thing is that I'm pretty sure he's serious about it."

"I don't know that I would want to have Matt Roberts as my dad."

"He can be a little intimidating sometimes," Caridad conceded.

"And you can't?" Miranda teased.

Caridad shrugged. "Totally different."

"Yup, totally. Matt will just drill you with a ninety-five mile per hour fastball, whereas you're just constantly armed."

"Hey! I've only had to draw my gun in self defense once,

and quite frankly that was more than enough."

Miranda rubbed Caridad's shoulder and squeezed. "Sorry. I wasn't thinking."

She waved a hand dismissively. "It's okay. All I can say is thank God for therapy."

"I can't even imagine what that must have been like."

"Kind of scary, to be quite honest, but nothing I wouldn't do again if I had to."

Miranda got up to grab a drink from the cooler sitting just outside the circle of chairs. She was debating between a beer or Dr. Pepper when felt a presence beside her and looked up.

Darrin was standing just a foot away, a casual grin on his face and his hands stuffed into the pockets of jeans that probably cost more than her entire monthly salary. His t-shirt had the appearance of being well-worn, but she suspected he'd paid big bucks to buy one that looked that way.

She barely managed to not look down at her own outfit of faded boyfriend jeans and a purple tank top.

Both bought from Wal-Mart.

"Care to hand me a beer?"

She blinked owlishly. "Uh, sure. What kind?"

"What do we have?"

She peered back into the cooler. "Looks like Shiner, Lone Star, and something I've never seen before."

"I guess I'll try the one you've never seen before."

"Sure thing." Sure thing? Jeez, she sounded like the biggest dork who'd ever dorked in the history of ever.

Mentally shaking herself she grabbed one of the unfamiliar bottles and a Shiner. She was suddenly feeling the urge to drink her thoughts away.

Not that she would.

But the urge was there.

She closed the cooler and stood, handed Darrin his bottle. Their fingers brushed in the exchange, and the sensation caused excitement to flutter in her tummy.

On second thought maybe she didn't need alcohol after all

because clearly her imagination—and hormones—was going off the rails.

She stood there like an idiot for what felt like forever, but was probably only seconds. At any rate, it was more than long enough to make her uncomfortably aware of her awkwardness and Darrin's hotness.

She scrunched her nose and took a step backwards.

"I don't smell bad, do I?"

"Uh, no. Of course not." She swallowed. "I'm just gonna so sit back down now."

She barely refrained from running back to her seat. She plopped down and looked at her beer, realizing she'd run away before popping the top off on the cooler's attached bottle opener.

She was halfway out of her chair when Caridad whispered, "It's a twist top."

Miranda looked down and sure enough, it was a twist top. Didn't she just feel like an idiot? "Thanks."

Caridad leaned over and, her voice still a whisper, said, "For the record, I think he's attracted to you, too."

She choked on her beer and took a few sputtering breaths before saying, "Excuse me?"

"You know exactly what I'm talking about."

"Ummm…"

Caridad snorted, but her voice remained at a whisper. "Seriously. He's been watching you all night, and he didn't even bother to get up and get a drink until you did."

Miranda rolled her eyes. "What are we, in high school?"

"Dating can sometimes seem that way."

"Who said anything about dating?"

"Semantics." Caridad took a drink of her own beer before continuing. "A word of caution, though—unless you're looking for casual I wouldn't even try to go there. Not that he's a bad guy—he's actually a fantastic friend—he just doesn't seem to be remotely interested in something serious."

Miranda chuckled. "As if I'm looking for anything at

all—serious or casual."

Caridad's expression turned serious. "And that's fine. I just happened to notice some sparks and since I like both of you I figured I would give you fair warning."

"Fair enough." She tapped her foot against the limestone patio and slowly sipped from her beer bottle. After long moments of silence she said quietly, "Besides, I seriously doubt I'm his type anyway."

Caridad threw back her head and laughed. "I knew it!"

"Shh!"

She quieted her laughter before saying, "No, you're not his usual type. From where I'm sitting, though, that's not necessarily a bad thing."

Miranda gazed into the fire. "Not that it matters anyway. Because, like I said, I'm not interested nor do I have the time."

"Yeah, keep telling yourself that, chica."

Darrin watched Miranda and Caridad from across the fire pit while pretending to pay attention to Matt. From the furtive glances Caridad was shooting his way—not to mention the fact that Miranda was obviously not looking his way—he could only guess that they were talking about him.

In any other circumstance he probably would have been annoyed, but he was too amused at the thought of Caridad gossiping to let it get to him. Moving back home and meeting Owen had definitely been good for her.

Miranda, on the other hand...he got the distinct impression that he made her uncomfortable, but he couldn't for the life of himself figure out why.

Okay, if he was honest with himself he could figure out why. But so what if he was one of the ranch's owners? He was pretty much a silent partner and saw it as an investment and nothing more. He knew squat about wildlife management and hunting, so he was more than happy to provide money and let Chase and Owen handle the day to day stuff.

Besides, he had his hands full with work anyway.

"Dude. Have you even heard a word I've said in the past five minutes?" Matt lightly shoved his shoulder.

Darrin shook his head as if to clear it. "Sorry. My mind wandered. What's up?"

"I was telling you that Everett texted me earlier. He made the twenty-five man roster."

Darrin smiled. Thomas Everett was the Wranglers' rookie outfielder and one of Darrin's newest clients thanks to Matt. "He's obviously stoked—his word, not mine."

"I take it you were able to negotiate a favorable contract for everyone involved?"

"Of course. To be fair, though, this one was pretty easy—Everett's going to be a star and the Wranglers needed a new outfielder."

"Truth. He's a good kid, too, which is always a plus. Smart. Hard worker."

Darrin chuckled. "You're not officially the player liaison yet, man."

"I know. I figured it doesn't hurt to get some practice in, though."

After retiring in October, the Wranglers offered Matt what was essentially a brand new position—Player Liaison—to not only keep him within the organization but to also help provide a line of communication between the front office and the players. They'd officially signed on the dotted line a week ago, but Matt wouldn't be starting until after Chase's kidney transplant.

"This position was literally made for you. You'll be fine."

Matt shrugged a shoulder. "Oh, I know. I'm just happy for Everett. For some reason the kid's taken a liking to me."

"He doesn't strike me as a glutton for punishment, but you never know."

"He's a Stanford grad—so obviously it's nothing more than his superior intellect."

Darrin laughed and took a drink of his beer. Damn, it was

good to be around friends again.

"I still can't believe you're getting married and having a baby."

Matt grinned. "Me, either. I'm one lucky SOB, though."

"Damn straight you are." His gaze slid to Miranda and Caridad, who had their heads together and were whispering to each other. "Think Owen and Caridad will be next?"

Matt scratched his chin. "I'm not sure, honestly."

"Trouble in paradise?"

"No, nothing like that. More that I get the feeling she wants to take things slow and he's willing to buy a ring yesterday."

"Caridad can be a tough nut to crack. My money's on Owen, though."

"Seriously? You've seen how good she is with a gun, right?"

Darrin smiled. "Yup. But Owen has the patience of a saint and loves her, therefore my money's on him."

"Fair enough. What about you?"

Darrin looked down at the beer in his hand. "What about me?"

"Got anyone special back in Dallas?"

He snorted. "Come on, Matt, you know me better than that."

"Dude. One night stands get kind of old after a while."

He raised an eyebrow. "Seem to me they keep things exciting."

"For a little while. Believe me when I say, though, that sex with someone you love is amazing. I always thought the term 'making love' was fucking corny, but with Jenn? It's so far beyond corny."

"TMI."

"Whatever. TMI would be telling you her favorite position—which is none of your goddamned business."

"Not that I want to know anyway."

"Good answer. But seriously. You really should try to find

someone worth settling down with, or at least committing to."

"I'll get right on that, Dr. Ruth." His tone was dry. "Can we not talk about my love life anymore? I'm starting to feel like an old woman at a sewing circle."

"Do you even know what a sewing circle is?"

"Um, a circle of women sitting around sewing?"

"I didn't realize they taught that in the pages of GQ."

"Yeah, fuck off," he said without heat, causing Matt to throw back his head and laugh.

"I am so glad you were able to make it."

Darrin took a swig of his beer and swallowed before saying, "Me too."

CHAPTER SEVEN

As a kid, what did you want to be when you grew up?

LATER THAT NIGHT, LONG AFTER EVERYONE ELSE HAD TURNED IN, Miranda grabbed her tripod and camera and made her way outside. It was one of those absolutely clear nights where the stars sparkled like a blanket of diamonds in the sky, and the moon hung low and fat.

She set her equipment on the edge of the patio, giving herself an unobstructed view of the night sky. Once she had the camera positioned and the shutter speed slowed down, she hooked up the remote and sat down in one of the Adirondack chairs.

"You sure don't see stars like this in the city."

The remote flew out of her hand and she barely stifled a scream at the unexpected sound of Darrin's voice. Hand over her racing heart, she said, "Jesus, you scared me."

She peered into the night shadows, trying to figure out where he was.

"Sorry. I didn't mean to startle you."

There. To her right. She finally made out the shadowy silhouette of a man. A man that was apparently walking towards her.

"Yeah, well, you shouldn't be hiding out in the dark like that." She sounded snippy, but dammit her heart was still racing and she'd just about had a year scared off of her life.

He drew near enough for her to barely make out the features of his face. His mouth was drawn into a flat line. "I really didn't mean to scare you."

She took a deep breath and looked away, grateful for the darkness that should at least somewhat help hide her reaction to him. "Sorry for sounding so snippy."

She picked up the remote and settled back into her chair.

Instead of going away like she'd kind of hoped he would, he dragged a chair over and sat next to her. Not entirely sure why he'd done so, she decided to keep her mouth shut and wait him out.

"You really don't see stars like this in the city," he finally said, repeating his earlier statement.

She decided to accept the verbal olive branch and said, "You don't see stars like this anywhere."

He probably already thought she was an outdoorsy country bumpkin, so she wasn't about to further tarnish her image by geeking out on him about astronomy.

"I think I remember reading somewhere that this area of south Texas is the darkest in the lower forty-eight."

"It's because of the lack of light pollution."

Okay, so maybe she was going to geek out just a little bit.

"It is definitely dark out here. I can't figure out if it's peaceful or creepy."

She snorted. "It's probably not for everybody."

"You obviously love it."

"What makes you say that?"

"You could have chosen to stay in town rather than move out here. Besides, the nighttime photography kind of gives you away."

"Fair enough." How was that for scintillating conversational skills? Ugh.

"So what exactly are you photographing?"

"I'm trying to get the moon in all of its phases."

"Why?"

"Because I can?"

"Sorry. I mean, is this just for fun or is it something more professional?"

"A little bit of both." She hesitated before continuing. "At the risk of boring you to tears, I'm trying to track the nocturnal habits of wildlife, along with activity level during different phases of the moon and weather patterns. Basically, I have game cams set up in various places to capture photos so I can reference the lunar phase, brightness of the night sky, etc."

"So what exactly will all of that tell you?"

She shrugged. "I'm honestly not sure yet. A lot of hunters believe that whitetail activity ebbs and flows with the lunar cycle, and there's some research out there to support that theory. I'm interested in seeing how all of the wildlife behaves during certain times of the month, especially since I've caught a mountain lion roaming around recently."

"What have you found so far?"

She laughed. "So far I've found a whole lot of nothing. This time of year the deer tend to be more nocturnal anyway because of the cooler night time lows and warmer day time high temperatures. If we still have any bears around we'll hopefully start picking those up fairly soon on the game cams. So far the mountain lion's the most exciting thing, and I'm trying to get as much data on it as I can before it moves on."

"Did you just say bears?"

"Yes."

"As in those big things that hibernate and can kill a grown ass man with one swipe of its claws?"

"As in bears. Yes."

"I didn't even know Texas had bears. What kind are they?"

"Black bears. They're actually smaller than the bears people usually think of—like grizzly bears—and used to be all over this part of the state."

"Really? What happened to them?"

"Are you seriously interested in this?"

"Absolutely. I'm a fan of learning new things."

"Okay then…well, like I said, they used to be plentiful but hunting and loss of habitat really caused their numbers to dwindle. They're now an endangered species and thanks to conservation efforts—and a couple of years' worth of good rain—they're making a bit of a comeback. We had a mama bear here last summer. She stuck around in one of the caves until her cub was old enough to follow her and they disappeared. I'm assuming they're still alive, mostly because that's what I want to believe."

He drummed his fingers on the wooden arm of his chair. "You obviously love animals."

"Yes."

He drummed his fingers some more. "So how do you reconcile that with working for a hunting ranch?"

"Have you ever hunted before?" she asked instead of directly answering his question.

"Honestly? No."

"And yet you partially own a hunting ranch."

"It seemed like a solid investment."

"Why did it seem like a solid investment?"

"Because they're not exactly making more land. That, and after looking at the data on how much money is pumped into the hunting industry every year it seemed like a no-brainer."

"So it's about the long-term investment?"

"Absolutely."

"Hunting and wildlife conservation go hand-in-hand for the long-term benefits of the herd and the land. Take whitetails for example. Down here in south Texas we're overrun with them. The land itself can only sustain so many, so when those numbers get out of whack it can cause the herd to be unhealthy due to a lack of resources.

"With axis, for example, they're not even an indigenous species and they compete with native animals for habitat and resources. Thus, their numbers definitely need to be managed.

"And then there's the wild hog issue. They reproduce like crazy, and cause millions of dollars worth of damage every year. They're also a non-native species that has managed to flourish.

"There are also predators—like mountain lions, coyotes, foxes, and bobcats—that also need to be kept in check. Obviously, nature does a pretty good job of sorting itself out—it's that whole survival of the fittest thing—but when you have humans and wildlife and, say, livestock coexisting, it's a very delicate balance. The most responsible way of maintaining that balance is through hunting—the population and herd health is controlled and someone fills their freezer with meat for their family. It's a win-win in my book."

"So that's how I get your eyes to sparkle—get you talking about wildlife conservation"

She looked away, embarrassed and glad for the low light that hopefully hid her flushed cheeks. "Sorry. I'm kind of passionate about what I do."

"I get that. Even though what I do probably isn't anywhere near as important as what you do, I love it."

"How do you even get into that career field?" she asked, glad to have the attention deflected off of her.

"I played sports all through junior high and high school—baseball, football, basketball. I even ran track. I was athletic, but not talented enough to be able to play at a collegiate, much less professional, level. But I loved sports."

"So why not coach?"

He chuckled. "My dad asked me the same thing; I think he was hoping I would come back home and teach at my high school. To be honest, though, I just can't see myself coaching. I don't know that I have the temperament for it."

Her brows drew together. "Why do you say that?"

"Being an agent…it's just different. There's a certain amount of throat cutting that goes on. If you're teaching kids, I don't think parents would appreciate a blood-thirsty coach."

"Clearly you've never seen Varsity Blues."

"I don't want your life," he quipped, making her laugh.

"That might have been the worst Jonathon Mox impression I've ever heard."

She barely made out his shrug in the moonlight. "Sorry. Even I can't imitate James Van Der Beek's bad Texas accent."

"It was bad, wasn't it?"

"Unbelievably so."

She looked up at the twinkling night sky and hit the trigger on the remote. In the brief quiet she could hear the faraway yip of a coyote and the familiar sound of fronds rubbing against each other in the gentle night breeze.

Yes, she could have decided to stay in town and make the drive up here every day, but she wouldn't have gotten to experience this. At least, not on a regular basis.

She loved Trevor with everything in her, and she generally wasn't the type to complain when she'd been the one who'd had unprotected sex. As her grandmother had been fond of saying, she'd made her bed and now she had to lay in it.

And she had.

But there were times—like now—when she was acutely aware of her status as Trevor's Mom. Nights like this, sitting outside under the stars and just enjoying the peace and quiet, hadn't happened before this job. Sometimes she felt selfish— she knew Trevor missed his friends in town—but she'd somehow gained friends while technically being more isolated.

And dammit, just because she was Trevor's Mom that didn't mean she stopped being Miranda Jacobson.

Unfortunately, that was something she usually had a hard time remembering.

Right now, though, the two identities were warring inside of her. As Miranda, she was appreciating the company of an attractive man who kept flirting with her. As Trevor's Mom, she was wary of even enjoying the attention, much less reacting on her baser urges and going beyond flirtation.

Her thoughts battling each other in her head, she continued to look up at the stars, feeling small and a little lost. She wasn't entirely sure she liked it, either.

CHAPTER EIGHT

What's your ideal first date spot?

"I MADE THIRTY MILLION DOLLARS LAST YEAR AND YOU EXPECT ME to hang this frou frou crap from the rafters?"

Jenn sighed at her future husband and said, "It's called tulle. And no, I don't want it hanging from the rafters, just draped across the arch."

Matt looked down at the gauzy fabric in his hands, a look of bewildered resignation on his face. Miranda somehow managed not to laugh.

"The things I'll do for love," Matt muttered.

Jenn smirked. "I promise it won't emasculate you."

"Right." He stomped over to the arch and proceeded to drape the white tulle in a way that would have made David Tutera proud.

"Sometimes I think he just likes to argue in the hopes he'll get make up sex," Jenn mumbled as she went back to arranging flowers in Mason jars.

Miranda did laugh at that. "Men have such one track minds."

"Women can, too." Jenn's grin was full of joyous mischief.

She wouldn't know about make up sex and one track

minds, so instead of responding she continued to set chairs around the tables they'd dragged into the barn that morning.

"I can't believe you're so calm—or that you're working on your wedding day."

"Eh, there's no point in being nervous. I'm marrying the only man I've ever loved and the father of my soon-to-be-born daughter. It's a little too late for cold feet now."

"You know you don't have to get married just because you're preggo, right?"

Jenn threw back her head and laughed. "Have you met Matt? He's about as traditional as they come, no matter how hard he tries not to show it. Besides, we're not getting married just because I'm pregnant—that's just a happy coincidence."

"I know—I just wanted to give you a chance to back out while you still could." She grinned.

"Well, I thank you for the opportunity, but there's no way in hell I'm backing out at this point; you heard him say how much he brought in last year." Jenn winked, making Miranda chuckle.

She didn't think it mattered one bit to Jenn how much money Matt had made last year, but she had to admit the amount was mind boggling. She was pretty sure she wouldn't ever make that much in her entire lifetime—much less in one year.

Matt muttered something unintelligible to himself as he walked out of the barn, making Miranda shake her head and smile.

This was sure to be one interesting wedding.

When all was said and done, the wedding was small but beautiful. Jenn had been glowing in a soft-looking wedding dress that proudly accentuated her baby bump. Matt had been handsome—as if he would ever be capable of being anything but hotness personified—in his dove gray suit.

There had been tears and laughter during their wedding

vows, and now the sun was sinking below the horizon as guests danced, ate cake, and drank wine or beer. Dinner had been a delicious selection of wild game harvested from the ranch; juicy wild hog, venison kabobs, and dove from last season that had been stuffed with cream cheese and jalapeños then wrapped in bacon before being cooked on the smoker. It had all been served with baked beans, peppered corn, rolls, a delicious spring mix salad, and sweet tea.

It had been heavenly.

In keeping with the not exactly traditional wedding food, Matt and Jenn had opted to have just one cake—a delicious tuxedo truffle cake. Miranda was seriously debating getting a second piece, even if she was already stuffed.

Screw it. That was really good cake.

"Care to dance?"

Darrin suddenly appearing right in front of her brought her up short.

"Um…I was actually just about to grab a piece of cake."

His smile caused nerves and butterflies to dance in her tummy.

The man really was too potent for his own good.

"Just one dance?"

His expression was so hopeful she couldn't turn him down.

Plus, it would be rude to not dance with him just this one time, considering she'd danced with pretty much everyone else so far tonight.

"Okay. Just one."

In that way that DJs always seemed to do, the music changed just seconds after Darrin had wrapped his arms around her, from something that was slightly up-tempo to the grandaddy of them all.

Boys II Men.

She felt like she'd suddenly stepped into a 1990s romcom.

"This song is like a flashback to junior high," Darrin said, kind of echoing her thoughts.

"No kidding."

"If I had known this song was going to start playing…"

"It's a wedding. No worries," she said, cutting him off.

"Fair enough. But still…"

She dragged her gaze away from the button it had been glued on since they'd stepped onto the dance floor and up to his face.

"Seriously, it's okay." The look on his face was too intense. Too male. Too sexy. Too everything. So she dropped her gaze back down to that stupid button and swallowed the lump of emotion that had lodged itself in her throat.

Unfortunately, shutting her mouth only allowed her brain to pick up on the party her hormones were apparently throwing.

Her stomach dipped and rolled, and her limbs felt heavy and prickly with awareness. Her nipples were hard against the cotton of her bra, and her sex felt swollen and achy.

The last time she'd felt any of those things had been before she'd found out she was pregnant.

Well, at least, in the presence of a man.

She didn't have time for physical attraction. She didn't want to be attracted to Darrin—her focus needed to be on Trevor and her job. Nothing more, nothing less.

Especially since when the weekend was over Darrin would go back up to Dallas and she'd most likely never see him again.

And suddenly it was just too much.

The song came to a merciful end, and she stepped away like she'd just burned her hand on a hot stove.

"Uh, thanks. For the dance," she said before walking out of the barn.

Air, she needed air.

She was barely five feet away from the door when Darrin's hand on her elbow stopped her and spun her around so that they were once again face to face, body to body.

And just like that, all of her thoughts flew out the proverbial window.

CHAPTER NINE

What types of women do you typically gravitate towards?

"THIS ISN'T HAPPENING, DARRIN," SHE SAID, HOLDING UP HER hand in an effort to stop him and gather herself.

"What isn't happening?"

She closed her eyes briefly. Lord, give me strength.

"This, Darrin. You. Me."

His hand flexed on her hip, and Miranda took a step back, needing to put distance between them.

Self-preservation and all that.

"Why not?"

Oh, for the love of… "Because you're my freaking boss!"

"I'm not technically your boss—Chase and Owen are."

"That's beside the point. You're one of the owners, so you're partially responsible for my paycheck and the roof over my and my son's heads. Therefore, this is a line that will not and cannot be crossed."

"I have nothing to do with the day to day running of this ranch, and you know it."

"That's beside the point. You're still an owner. That's more than enough for me."

"So you won't even let me kiss you because I'm silent owner, but you'll let Trevor think of the other three owners—and their significant others—as his uncles and aunts?"

"That's totally different and you know it."

"No, I don't. Please explain."

A sound of frustration escaped her lips and Miranda barely managed to not yank at her hair. "It's different because we've known Chase, Owen, and Matt since before I became an employee here. The personal relationship was established long before the employee/employer relationship."

"You want to know what I think?"

"Not really."

"Too bad, because I'm telling you anyway."

She sighed.

"I think you're just using the fact that you're an employee as an excuse to keep your distance."

Well, no shit.

"And I think you're just as attracted to me as I am to you, and that scares you."

She raised an eyebrow. "I've faced down mountain lions scarier than you."

Okay, that was only partially true. Sure, she'd faced down a mountain lion before, but she'd also been armed and able to defend herself then, unlike now.

His body crowded in on hers, and too late she noticed that he'd somehow managed to maneuver them away from the other wedding guests and to the side of the barn. The sounds of voices and music wafted out of the building, and the slight April breeze drifted over her bare arms, causing her to shiver.

Her back met cool metal. She swallowed nervously.

Darrin tucked a strand of hair behind her ear and said softly, "I don't get it."

"Get what?"

"Why I want you so bad."

"Well, if you were trying to warm me up that was an epic fail."

He chuckled. "That came out wrong. I know why I want you physically—you're beautiful."

"But?"

"But we're from two completely different worlds."

"You think? You're Armani and five-star restaurants, and I'm dirt and homemade spaghetti. Your days are spent rubbing elbows with the rich and famous and mine are spent counting deer and making maps."

"It's oddly fascinating."

"You sure do know how to flatter a girl."

"I didn't think you wanted me to flatter you."

"I don't."

"Oh, I think you do."

He placed his palms on the side of the barn, caging her in. "Not really. No."

"I'm going to kiss you now."

"I don't think—" before she could finish her sentence, his lips were on hers, soft and warm. Gentle.

Her body melted into the barn against her will, and his lips moved over hers in featherlight touches that only left her wanting more.

She bit back a sound of frustration. His mouth grew more insistent, his tongue teasing her lips until she opened to him.

Her hands snaked up around his neck, pressing his head closer as the kiss turned more demanding. Hotter. Wetter.

How had she forgotten how much she loved kissing? Once upon a time, kissing had been one of her favorite past times; there was just something about the act that she'd adored as a teenager and young woman. Since Trevor had been born, though, she'd sublimated those needs and wants and had allowed herself to forget how joyful the simple intimacy could be.

Darrin's body pressed against hers, and she could feel him hard against her belly through their clothes. Warning bells went off in her head.

Just a little longer.

It had been so, so long since she'd been kissed and she wasn't quite willing yet to stop.

The warning bells kept going off, though, and they finally

pierced through her brain fog just enough for her to realize the sound wasn't just in her head. She broke the kiss and said, "I think you're ringing."

Darrin shook his head. "Not me. My phone's on vibrate." He swooped in for another kiss.

The bells kept ringing. She pulled away again. "Then where the hell is that noise coming from?"

Just as she finished her question, she realized the sound was coming from the pocket of her dress.

Trevor must have been playing with her phone at some point, she thought, since the ring tone wasn't one she recognized. She grabbed the phone and checked the caller ID, frowning at the display.

"What's wrong?"

She typed in her passcode and opened the trail cam app that had suddenly started going haywire.

"I'm not sure. One of my new game cams just started going bonkers."

"You get cell phone messages from a game cam?"

She glanced up at him before looking back down at her phone. "Uh, yeah. The technology's been around for a few years now."

"Huh. That's pretty cool. So what's going on?"

As the grid of photos loaded, a chill snaked down Miranda's spine.

Panic threatened to rise up and take over, but she stuffed it down and pushed away from Darrin, marching towards one of the UTVs that was parked behind the barn. Caliche crunched under her flats, and she nonsensically thought that these shoes were so not appropriate for what she was about to have to do.

Hysterical laughter bubbled up her throat, and she swallowed it, silencing it and the fear that wanted to pulse through her veins.

"Miranda? What's wrong?" Darrin asked from beside her.

"Go get Owen and Daniel. Tell them to bring rifles and Walkie Talkies to Tall Boy. They'll know what I'm talking about," she said as she checked the gun boot on the Ranger to make sure her rifle was still in it. She then slid behind the wheel, opened the glove box and saw that the 44 Magnum revolver she kept in it was also there and fully loaded with a box of ammo sitting beside it. She pressed her foot to the brake and turned the key, starting the UTV. As she put it into Drive she turned to Darrin and said, "And tell them to hurry," before hitting the gas and speeding off into the setting sun.

Darrin watched as Miranda sped off in the utility vehicle, feeling frozen in place for a brief second before turning quickly on his heel and jogging into the barn. As inconspicuously as possible he searched the barn for Daniel and Owen, finding the two men and Caridad standing close to the open bar. He made his way over to them and cut Daniel off mid-sentence. "Sorry to interrupt, guys, but you apparently need to get to something called Tall Boy ASAP with walkie talkies and rifles."

"What's going on?" Daniel asked.

Darrin shrugged. "I have no idea. Miranda's phone started going crazy with a bunch of alerts from a trail cam she'd just put up. She turned white as a ghost then took off in one of the UTVs."

"Shit," Daniel said.

"Where's Trevor?" Darrin asked, looking around for the little boy to make sure someone kept an eye on him for the next however long this took.

Caridad and Owen looked around, too.

"The last time I saw him he was eating cake," Caridad said.

"I'm not seeing him," Darrin said, dread pooling in the pit of his stomach. "You don't think he might have gone back to the house, do you?"

Daniel shook his head. "No. That kid loves to be around people. Maybe he's playing with Winchester somewhere?"

He didn't sound hopeful, either.

"I've got a bad feeling about what that trail camera picked up, guys," Darrin said, swallowing the lump of dread in his throat.

"Well, then, let's get to it," Owen said before heading towards the front of the barn, Daniel, Darrin, and Caridad on his heels.

They made a quick stop at Daniel's office in between the barn and the house, and Daniel came back out with two rifles slung over his shoulders and a holster slung low on his hips, holding a revolver. Owen held four walkie talkies in his hands and cradled a first aid kit under his arm. "Let's go," he said, leading them to a large Ranger that looked like it could hold about eight people.

They climbed in, Daniel taking the wheel and Owen the front passenger seat. Darrin and Caridad slid onto the back seat and braced themselves as Daniel started the UTV and took off.

Please be okay. Please be okay. Please be okay.

The words ran through Miranda's head on a loop as she sped towards Tall Boy, which was the tallest hunting blind on the ranch. How Trevor and Winchester had gotten that far in such a short amount of time was beyond her, considering she didn't think she'd been outside with Darrin for that long.

Served her right, though, and pretty much proved her point that she and Darrin did not need to get involved with one another; she turned her attention away from Trevor for a few minutes and her baby—her fucking world—had wandered off into the scrub brush and cactus and was apparently being stalked by a mountain lion.

No, she definitely would not be kissing Darrin again.

As she rounded the sendero and drew closer to Tall Boy, she kept her eyes peeled for any sign of Trevor, Winchester, or the mountain lion. The sun had set at some point between her jumping in the Ranger and getting to this point, which meant there was only about twenty minutes of low light left before everything went pitch black.

Her heart pounded in her chest and the spit in her mouth turned as dry as sawdust at the thought of her son out here at night by himself with a mountain lion definitely in the area.

She got to Tall Boy and slowed to look around before following the sendero in the direction Trevor and Winchester were heading according to the photos from the game cam. She looked at her watch and saw that the time between receiving the photos and getting here was all of eight minutes, so Trevor and Win should be fairly close by.

She hoped.

She drove for a couple more minutes before stopping the Ranger and cutting the ignition in order to see if she could hear anything that would clue her in as to where her son was. She was just reaching into the glove box for the revolver when the unmistakable cry of a mountain lion filled the air, making her blood run cold and her stomach pitch and heave. She stuffed a box of ammo into one of her dress pockets and was sliding out of the Ranger when she heard the deep, unmistakable sound of Winchester barking. She'd been around him—and other Great Pyrenees—enough to know it was his "I mean business" bark.

Miranda retrieved the AR from the gun boot and made sure it was loaded. She slung it over her shoulder before forcing herself to stand still and listen in order to get a better idea of where Trevor, Win, and the mountain lion were. As much as she wanted to charge in, guns blazing, she knew that doing so without having a good idea of where the cougar was in relation to her son could breed nothing but trouble and heartache.

Her heart pounded as she waited, silently praying. She could hear the sound of an engine coming closer. Backup was on its way.

She hoped like hell she didn't need it.

She'd just opened her mouth to shout out to Trevor when another bone-chilling cry pierced the air, about two hundred yards to the left if she was guessing correctly.

Another series of deep barks followed, a little further away but also to the left.

The light was fading fast, and she hastily grabbed a flashlight from the bed of the Ranger before taking off towards the barking that had become continuous and interspersed with deep growls.

As she picked her way through cactus, scrub brush, and oak trees she cocked the hammer on the revolver with her thumb, mentally preparing herself to bring the gun up and fire at a moment's notice should she have to.

After what seemed like hours but was probably no more than a few minutes, she emerged from the thick scrub brush and into a clearing she recognized from the typography mapping she'd been doing over the past couple of months; it held one of a handful of small, spring-fed pools that bubbled up from under the ground. It was a popular drinking ground for the ranch's wildlife large and small, which would explain the mountain lion's presence.

The mountain lion that was currently about fifteen yards from her son and her boss's dog, fangs bared and ready to spring.

Winchester's deep barks pierced the evening air, keeping the big cat at a distance. The Pyr had placed himself between the cougar and Trevor—who was pressed tightly against an oak tree, tears streaming down his face and a dark stain rapidly spreading across the front of his pants.

The sight made her want to cry, too.

Instead, she slowly set the revolver down on the ground and shouldered the rifle. She clicked the safety off as the cougar sniffed the air and turned its head towards her, its yellow green eyes almost glowing in the low light. Heart pounding and palms sweating, she put the crosshairs of the rifle's scope on the mountain lion and pulled the trigger. The big cat lurched forward, and she quickly took a second shot, this one causing the cougar to fall to the ground, its chest heaving mightily as its back legs twitched before finally going still.

Winchester inched closer to the lion and growled. She kept the rifle trained on the cougar and shouted, "Trevor, honey, stay where you are until we're sure he's dead, okay?"

Her son sniffled and in between sobs choked out, "O—kk—ay."

Her heart twisted in her rib cage, hating to see her baby so shaken up.

He was so going to be grounded for at least a month after this little stunt.

"Miranda! Where are you?" Owen's voice carried on the still night air.

"Over here. About two hundred yards to the left of the Ranger. Follow the deer trail."

"Is everyone okay?" Daniel shouted out.

"A little scared, but unharmed," she shouted back.

Trevor sniffled again and he tried to tug his shirt down to cover the wetness saturating the front of his pants.

Okay, maybe he was only going to be grounded for three and a half weeks.

Winchester continued to inch closer to the mountain lion, sniffing in between growls. Slowly, the dog's posture began to relax and he growled one last time before turning around and sitting at Trevor's side. Trevor's knees buckled and he buried his face in the dog's neck. Miranda flipped the safety back on and slung the rifle back onto her shoulder before picking up the revolver and de-cocking it.

She heard a crashing sound to her right and looked up to see Owen, Daniel, Caridad, and Darrin emerge into the clearing a few yards away. They all stopped short when they saw the dead mountain lion, and Owen whistled low before saying, "No wonder you took off like you did."

"Is that what I think it is?" Darrin asked.

"If you think it's a mountain lion, then yes, it is what you think it is," Daniel said, a note of superiority in his voice.

Miranda rolled her eyes and walked over to Trevor, who she gathered in her arms and held tight.

"I'm so-sorry, Mama."

She smoothed a hand over his back. "Shh. You're okay. Don't ever run off like that again, though, okay?"

He nodded against her shoulder then pulled away. "You killed it!"

"I did, yes."

Winchester wedged his nose between them, and Trevor said, "Winchester kept it away."

"I know. I saw."

"Do you think he would have fought it?"

"Probably, if he had to. That's what Pyrs are bred to do."

Trevor scrunched up his nose. "They're supposed to kill mountain lions?"

She took a deep breath and asked for patience. "If they have to, yes. Now, how about we get you and Win back to the house?"

"But what about the mountain lion?"

"Don't worry, little man, we'll take care of it," Owen said.

"Are you going to bury it? If you do, it needs to have a funeral. That's what you do when something dies."

Oh her sweet, innocent boy. "No, it won't have a funeral, per se. We have to report it to the state, and I'll need to gather some data on it, too."

"Can I help?"

"I think you've helped more than enough for one night, Trev. Let's get you back to the house, okay?"

He nodded and she grabbed his hand with her free one. Winchester trotted along at Trevor's side. They stopped when they got to everyone else. She looked at Owen and Daniel and said, "Can y'all load it up and bring it back to the house? I'll need to get measurements and stuff and then call it in to Texas Parks and Wildlife."

"Will do. You want it in the other barn?" Daniel asked.

She smiled, glad he was still willing to jump in and help despite her turning down his impromptu proposal the other day. She also kind of wished she felt an iota of the attraction for him that she felt for Darrin.

"Yes. Thank you. Come on, Trevor." They made their way back to the Ranger without incident, and Winchester climbed onto the front seat and parked himself in between her and Trevor. Apparently her son had a new best friend.

Which meant she would probably end up getting him a dog some point soon.

Because she was a sucker.

But every kid needed a dog, right?

They drove back to the house silently, Winchester's heavy panting in her ear a reminder of what she'd been doing while her son had slipped away from the wedding reception.

Further proof Darrin was a bad idea—the moment she closed her eyes and took her attention off the thing that was most important to her, everything went to hell in a hand basket.

CHAPTER TEN

What's your favorite part of being a sports agent?

Caridad: Hey. You wanna come with us up to Dallas for Chase's transplant?

Miranda: Ummm…wouldn't that be intruding on a family thing?

Less than a minute after sending the text, her phone vibrated with an incoming call.

Caridad.

She rolled her eyes, a smile on her face.

"Did you seriously just say you would be intruding on a family thing?" Caridad asked in lieu of a greeting.

"Yes."

Her friend sighed. "I'm not sure if you've noticed, but with this group of friends they're all pretty much family. Which is weird, sure, but it's also kind of nice."

"No, I've definitely noticed that. It's just…I'm an employee."

"So? You're also a friend. To all of us. Plus, Chase's dog has adopted your son and Jenn's already married her daughter off to Trevor. I'm pretty sure that makes you family."

Fair enough. "I have a lot going on here."

"I know. What I don't know is why you're being so difficult."

She wasn't about to give Caridad the real reason.

Her friend continued. "And if it's about Darrin, I get it. I really do. But I still think everyone would love to have you there. I know I would."

And because Miranda understood Caridad, she knew that what Caridad was really asking was for her to be there for her. Chase, Matt, Jenn, Jo, and Owen were a tight-knight group who'd been friends for forever. Even though they'd opened their arms—and their hearts—to Caridad as Owen's girl-friend, she still felt a little bit like the odd girl out.

Miranda pinched the bridge of her nose and blew out a long breath. "When do we leave?"

The mood was surprisingly jovial considering Matt and Chase were both going under the knife in the morning.

Considering what they were being operated on for, though, it made a weird sort of sense.

Even though she hadn't been privy to all of the down and dirty details regarding Chase's health, she'd known him long enough to see he really was sick. In the past few months alone he looked like he'd lost about twenty pounds.

She hadn't known Jo as long as she'd known Chase and Owen, but the worried relief on her face was obvious. Matt was amazingly relaxed considering he was literally giving his brother an organ tomorrow. Jenn was all smiles, but Miranda suspected she was putting up a really good facade.

Hell, if she were pregnant and her husband was having major surgery the next day, she would have been worried out of her mind and a total basket case.

Meanwhile, Owen looked happy, but there was a hint of sadness in his eyes. Caridad seemed slightly uncomfortable—like she was struggling to feel as if she belonged. No wonder she'd wanted Miranda around for moral support.

And Darrin. Well, he looked just as sexy as he had the

last time she'd seen him, and completely at ease with his sur-roundings.

Which was a lot more than she could say—fancy pizza places weren't exactly her norm.

And Grimaldi's was definitely a little more uptown than she was used to. Matt, Darrin, and Caridad had all sworn by the place, though, so here they were in the back corner, gourmet pizzas spread out in front of them.

Darrin had ordered one with grilled chicken, pesto, and artichoke hearts, which in her mind symbolized everything they didn't have in common. She and Caridad had agreed on a mushroom, pepperoni, and ham pizza with extra garlic. Because, garlic. Matt and Owen had piled one high with meat—pepperoni, meatballs, Italian sausage, ham, and bacon—and Chase, Jo, and Jenn had opted for black olives, extra basil, and pepperoni on another one.

It was a lot of pizza.

Judging by how much food Matt could put away just by himself, though, it was probably barely enough.

"Where're your parents?" Owen asked, looking at Chase.

"Tomorrow's actually their anniversary, so we told them to go out and do something nice for themselves," Chase said.

"Reservations may or may not have been made in their name at their favorite place here in Dallas," Matt chimed in.

"I'm sure they were grateful," Owen said dryly, making the brothers both laugh.

"Actually, I'm pretty sure Bo and Sarah both wanted to strangle their offspring," Jenn said, a smile teasing her lips.

"Oh, they thought about it," Matt said.

"We just wanted to do something nice for them considering the year they've had. First, with Matt's head injury and then me with this."

"Not to mention the fact you've both gotten married and they're about to be grandparents," Jo said before sipping her water.

Miranda ate pizza as the conversation flowed around her,

having nothing to really contribute. She had an inkling Caridad felt the same way, considering how quiet she was. Darrin, too, was quiet, occasionally checking his phone and responding to what she guessed were incoming texts or emails.

She felt incredibly out of place.

But at least the pizza was good.

Darrin hadn't expected to see Miranda again—at least, not so soon. Not that he didn't want to see her—he'd certainly thought about her often enough over the past couple of weeks.

It was just that he couldn't forget her stricken expression when Trevor had disappeared. She'd definitely blamed herself—and by extension, him—for looking away for even a second and taking time just for her.

He'd grown up in a single-parent household, the oldest of four siblings. He might not have ever been in his dad's shoes, but he'd certainly played the role of parent more often than not while Dad had been at one of his jobs.

His mom had left when he was seven—just six months after his youngest sister had been born—and it wasn't until they were all out of the house that his dad had even thought about dating. He'd put his life on hold for eighteen years. Darrin didn't think doing so had made him any happier.

So he had an idea of the weight that was on Miranda's shoulders.

He simultaneously wanted to carry it for her and leave her to it and walk away.

He supposed that made him a selfish bastard, but his world wasn't necessarily conducive to having a family life, either.

He happened to look up at the same time Miranda did. Their gazes caught and held; her eyes were filled with an uncertain turmoil he knew all too well.

Tension hung in the air between them, and her tongue sneaked out to wet her lips. His gaze followed the movement, heat shooting to his groin as he remembered what those lips and tongue had tasted like.

A sharp elbow in the ribs broke his concentration. He turned his head to the side, looking away from Miranda.

Caridad elbowed him again and dropped her voice so that only he could hear her. "Dude. Anymore of that and we're gonna have to start charging a cover price of nine ninety-nine."

"What?" he asked, confused.

Caridad rolled her eyes. "All the eye-fucking. It's like watching pay-per-view porn or something."

"Like you have any room to talk. You would throw Owen down on this table right now if you could."

She took a sip of her tea. "The difference, though, is that I'm not engaging in ocular fornication with my boyfriend in a public place."

He almost choked on his pizza, causing everyone to peer at him, concerned. He held up a hand to indicate he was okay while trying really hard not to glare at Caridad.

Owen's sharp gaze looked between the two of them and a wry smile twisted his mouth. "What inappropriate comments are you making now?"

Caridad blushed—actually blushed, which he hadn't known she was capable of—and said, "I was just telling him the story about everyone catching Sandy and Ted going at it in the restroom at my last match."

"Man, you three-gunners are kind of crazy," Matt said.

Caridad casually sipped her tea before saying, "Not three gun this time. IDPA. I hear the cowboy action folks get really crazy, though."

"Seriously?" Miranda asked.

Darrin had no idea what cowboy action was, but the visual that popped into his head was certainly…interesting.

"Oh, yeah. Those older folks definitely know how to have a good time."

And now he was picturing octogenarians dressed as cowboys and getting, well, some action.

It wasn't a pleasant image.

"How old are we talking here?" he asked, almost not wanting the answer.

Caridad shrugged. "Usually middle-aged and up, although there are some younger shooters starting to get into it."

Miranda asked, "Why haven't you? It's always looked fun to me."

Darrin's eyebrows rose of their own volition. Miranda must have noticed because she gave him a confused look and asked, "What?"

He lifted his hands in the air. "I didn't say anything."

"But you were clearly thinking something."

He shook his head. "Nope."

"Whatever." She looked away.

Matt coughed. "Anyway. Enough with the verbal foreplay, you two. I want to hear more about this Ted and Sandy situation."

Across the table, Miranda turned bright red and looked down at her plate. He would've punched his best friend if Matt wasn't giving away a freaking kidney in the morning.

Before anyone could respond to Matt, though, Thomas Everett walked up to their table and clapped Matt on the back.

"Why didn't you tell me you were in town, Old Man?" Thomas asked.

Matt stood and pulled Thomas in for a quick bro hug. "Spur of the moment decision, rookie."

Thomas, who was one of the smartest guys Darrin had ever represented, took a quick look around the table and lifted an eyebrow. "Right."

Not missing a beat, though, he smiled and said, "Hey, Jenn. Sorry I couldn't make it to the wedding and keep you from making a grave mistake."

Jenn laughed. "No worries, Thomas. I somehow managed to muddle through it on my own."

"You mean you didn't marry this loser?" he teased.

Jenn held up her left hand, showing off the sparkler Matt had given her on their wedding day. "Sorry to disappoint you."

Thomas whistled. "Day-um. Darrin over there's pretty good at negotiating contracts, but there's no way I could compete with that."

Everyone around the table laughed and Darrin said, "Give it time."

"Yeah, rookie," Matt added.

Thomas snorted. "Anyway. Hi, Chase. Hi, Jo. And hi everyone else. I just saw the Old Man here and thought I would come harass him for a minute. Have a nice evening." He flashed the megawatt smile female—and some male—Wranglers fans were already going gaga over and wandered back over to his own table.

Matt sat down and let out a breath.

"I take it the rookie doesn't know what's going on?" Owen asked.

Matt shook his head. "Nope. We've kept it quiet for now. The only people in the Wranglers organization who know what's going on are Reed Thornhill and HR. There's a reason why the news hasn't broke yet about my new position." He winked.

Chase and Matt both being former pitchers—and thus superstitious baseball players—had decided to not go public yet with the transplant story as a precautionary measure. Basically, neither of them wanted to jinx anything.

There was also the very obvious privacy issue; if local media were to find out the Wranglers' former ace was in the hospital, Baylor would turn into a media circus.

Hell, to be honest, Darrin was still amazed that they'd been able to keep any of it out of the news. The national sports media had been all over Matt's unlikely comeback story last year, and for a while there it had seemed like he couldn't even breathe without it being Tweeted about.

"You know he's gonna be pissed when he finds out what's really going on, right?" Chase asked his brother.

Matt shrugged. "Let him be pissed. He's a smart kid, he'll understand eventually. I'm not having this thing jinxed or turned into a media circus."

"I told you, Chase, you should've let me donate," Owen smirked.

Chase held up his hands. "Hey, I had nothing to do with that. They keep everything between the donor and recipient so separate the only way I knew what was going on was because of Matt giving me updates."

"They obviously knew my kidney would be superior so they worked me up first."

"Bullshit," Owen coughed into his hand. "We had blood drawn at the exact same time and we were both matches. You just happened to be a better match."

"Damn straight." Matt grinned. "Besides, he's getting a World Series Champion kidney. This thing's guaranteed to go the distance."

Caridad snorted and Jo mock-glared at her brother-in-law. "Don't you dare jinx this."

"I won't. Don't worry."

Darrin was pretty sure Jo was still worried. He didn't know her very well, but the tension in her shoulders and around her eyes was obvious to even the most casual observer.

The familiar banter was interrupted by their server bringing them the bill, which he and Matt argued over until Darrin finally just forced the server to take his card. Matt glared at him. Darrin laughed.

"Don't worry, Matt, he won't ever let me pay for anything, either," Caridad said.

"What's wrong with picking up the tab? Besides, I could technically classify this as a business dinner since two of my clients are sitting here."

"Hey, you won't hear me complaining, especially with some of the fancy places you like to eat at."

The server reappeared with the ticket and his card. Darrin tipped and signed the charge slip before putting the card back in his wallet. He knew Matt would probably be irritated with him for paying, but the way he saw it picking up the tab for dinner was the least he could do.

It wasn't like he'd been a match.

"Thanks, everyone, for being here," Chase said as they began to stand. "Y'all didn't have to be."

Owen raised a red eyebrow. "Where else would we have been?"

Chase shrugged, looking slightly uncomfortable. "Y'all are all taking time out of your lives to be here, and I know you all have plenty of other things you could be doing right now."

"Don't be a dumb ass," Owen said. "Nothing's more important than friends and family; everything else can wait."

CHAPTER ELEVEN

What's most important to you in life?

THE ALARM ON HER PHONE JOLTED MIRANDA OUT OF A DREAM IN which she'd been chasing down a pizza-covered mountain lion.

So freaking weird.

She turned off the alarm and rubbed her eyes, stretching under the cool, extremely soft cotton sheets in the guest room she'd been given. She guessed that multi-millionaire baseball players could probably afford luxury sheets.

Not that the sheets at the Devils Ranch were anything to sniff at—they definitely made sure guests and employees slept in style. But these sheets? They had to have like a bajillion thread count.

With a yawn she climbed out of bed and padded to the bathroom across the hall. After taking care of her morning business she jumped in the shower, letting her thoughts wander as warm water sluiced down her body.

Her eyes closed, and those thoughts jumped back to the night before. Seeing Darrin again had been slightly awkward and a lot frustrating. Despite the fear that had gripped her the night of Matt and Jenn's wedding, she hadn't been able to completely push that kiss from her mind.

Seeing him last night had brought the memory back front and center, and without the fear from that night gripping her she was able to admit—at least to herself—that she wouldn't mind it happening again.

Darrin's gaze on her had been hotly reserved; she'd been able to feel his continued interest, but he'd also barely acknowledged her. Not that she could blame him, considering how angry she'd been the last time they'd seen each other.

Speaking of Trevor, she really hoped he wasn't giving her parents too hard of a time this morning. Ever since the mountain lion incident he'd clung a little closer, to the point of refusing to go to school. She didn't know if it had simply scared him that much, of if there was something else going through his brain, but they'd had some epic battles the past couple of weeks.

If he didn't get beyond whatever it was soon, she was seriously considering taking him to a therapist. Which made her feel like a complete failure as a parent.

With a sigh she turned off the water and grabbed a towel. She dried herself off before wrapping it around her body and knotting it between her breasts. She cracked open the door, looked down the hall both ways, and crossed back to her bedroom after deeming the coast to be clear.

She dressed quickly, throwing on skinny jeans and a loose, flowy cotton top—something she didn't usually get to wear in her day-to-day life—before slipping her feet into a pair of deck shoes. If she was going to be sitting in a hospital all day, she was at least going to be comfortable.

Miranda exited the bedroom and made her way towards the kitchen and voices. Everyone was already gathered around the kitchen island, the smell of coffee lingering in the air. Matt and Chase were both drink-less, but everyone else was sipping from steaming mugs.

The mood was quiet and tense.

She poured herself a cup of coffee, added some sugar, and joined her friends at the island.

Caridad pushed a box of doughnuts towards her. "It's not the healthiest breakfast in the world, but it'll do for now."

Miranda shrugged and picked out a chocolate-glazed doughnut covered in sprinkles. "Mornings like these definitely call for sugar, I think."

"Truth," Jenn said and lifted a bear claw in a mock toast, "especially since I'm stuck with decaf until this baby comes out."

"That was one of the worst parts of being pregnant," Miranda said. "Well, aside from the whole baby daddy running away part. I wouldn't really recommend that to anyone."

Jenn turned to Matt. "Yeah, having that baby daddy around definitely makes things easier and less emotionally devastating."

Matt frowned. "Babe…"

Jenn waved her bear claw in the air. "I know. I'm not giving you a hard time or trying to make you feel bad. Just commiserating."

Matt wrapped his arm around his wife's waist and kissed the top of her head. "I was an idiot back then. Thank God you gave me a second chance."

"More like you forced me to give you a second chance." Jenn grinned before taking a bite of her pastry.

Miranda didn't know Matt and Jenn's entire story, just that they'd had a bit of a past and that it hadn't been all sunshine and roses. Despite that, though, there was no doubt that they absolutely adored one another.

Chase glanced down at his phone and then looked over at his brother. "Well, looks like we need to get going if we're going to be there on time."

Matt pushed away from the island. "Anyone want to take their coffee with them?"

Caridad and Miranda both answered in the affirmative, so Matt opened up a cabinet and handed them both a YETI Rambler. The two women poured their coffee into the cups, and Miranda topped hers off before popping on the lid.

Within minutes purses and bags were gathered, and soon they were all on their way to the Baylor University Medical Center campus just off of 175. Miranda, Owen, and Caridad all went in Owen's pickup, while Chase, Jo, Matt, and Jenn were all in Matt's JEEP.

Miranda hadn't been to Dallas in years, and the last time she'd been the traffic had been awful. Then again, compared to Del Rio all traffic was awful. This morning, though, their trip was smooth and quick, thanks to the early check-in time.

Once there, Matt pulled into valet parking in front of Jonsson Hospital, whereas Owen turned into a parking garage.

Less than ten minutes later, they were joining the other four in admissions.

She couldn't believe how calm both brothers appeared; she figured she would have been a nervous wreck had it been her either giving or receiving a kidney. Everyone made small talk, comments on the weather, the Wranglers' season so far, how light traffic had been, etc. until Chase and Matt's names were called, taking Jo and Jenn with them and leaving Owen, Caridad, and Miranda in the waiting area by themselves.

Caridad took a sip of her coffee then said, "Is it just me, or are they all unnaturally calm about this?"

Owen twirled a lock of Caridad's hair around his finger. "It's Chase and Matt. They're both fairly well known for staying cool under pressure."

"True. Then again, so am I, and I have to say I would be a nervous fucking wreck if I was in their shoes."

Miranda snorted, "No kidding. I couldn't imagine going through something like they are."

Owen's lips flattened into a straight line. "Me, either."

Caridad rubbed his arm and smiled at Miranda. "He's still feeling a little bitter about not being the donor."

"I'm not bitter," Owen said. "Besides, the way I look at it, if Chase ever needs another kidney somewhere down the line, we already know I'm a match. I'm basically Matt's reliever."

"I guess that's one way of looking at it," Miranda said

before taking a drink of coffee.

About fifteen minutes after they'd been taken back, the two couples reappeared with a registrar leading the way. Matt motioned for them to join them, so Miranda, Owen, and Caridad all got up and fell in line. They were taken to another waiting area in what was apparently a different hospital--these signs all said Roberts on them--where they were told to wait until it was time to go back into pre-op.

A few minutes after sitting down, Matt and Chase's parents, Bo and Sarah, walked in. Miranda had met them a handful of times and really liked them both, and even without knowing them all that well it was obvious that both parents were nervous and worried about their sons. As a mother herself, Miranda could imagine what it must be like, knowing both of your children were going to be operated on that day and that without said operation, one of those children would probably die.

The thought nearly took her breath away.

Moments later, Darrin showed up, once again wearing jeans that probably cost as much as her monthly salary, a light green polo shirt, and a sport jacket. He looked like the poster boy for Hot Businessmen Daily or something.

Greetings were exchanged, and once again the waiting and idle chit-chat began. Miranda's phone vibrated in her pocket, and she pulled it out to see a text from her mom.

A picture of a smiling Trevor greeted her, along with the message, "Love you Mom!"

She grinned and typed out a response.

Miranda: Love you, too, little man. Have a good day at school.

Mom: Ok. Granny put cookies in my lunch box.

Of course she had.

Miranda: And an apple, too, right?

Mom: ;P

Miranda: Be sure to eat the rest of your lunch. Not just the cookies.

Mom: k

She shook her head, a smile pulling at her lips. God, she loved that kid.

She was also pleasantly surprised that he seemed to be on his best behavior for his grandparents. Granted, his Granny's spoiling probably had a lot to do with that.

She was pulled from her thoughts by a nurse coming to get Matt to take him back to pre-op. The next few moments were filled with hugs and kisses and a few tears, and then Matt and Jenn were whisked away.

Chase exhaled and rubbed his hands over his face after he sat back down. Jo rubbed his back.

"This is really happening, isn't it?" he asked.

"Looks like it, Cowboy," Jo said.

Sarah sniffled and delicately blew her nose.

"Don't cry, Mom."

Sarah looked at her son incredulously. "How can I not cry? One of my sons needs a kidney to live and the other's giving him one so that he can. I'll cry if I damned well want to."

Chase held up his hands. "Fair enough."

"How long will it be before they come and get you?" Bo asked his youngest son.

He pushed a hand through his hair. "It's my understanding that they'll start getting Matt ready, and once he's almost ready to go back to the OR they'll come get me and get me ready. They'll start operating on him before they even take me back, so that they can take their time and examine the kidney to make sure it's viable before even opening me up. Once they know the kidney's good to go, they'll take me back and start operating."

Bo nodded and asked dryly, "So what you're saying is that we're going to be here for a while?"

Chase laughed. "Most likely. I mean, come on, Dad, it's a hospital."

A few minutes later another small group entered the waiting room, all of them wearing tired and nervous expressions.

She guessed that was probably normal; hospitals weren't exactly known for their relaxing atmospheres.

Not really having much to contribute to the conversation, she pulled her iPad out of her purse, figuring she could at least get some reading in.

She opened up the book she'd started a couple of days before and quickly became engrossed in the story.

She was pulled from her book some time later when the seat beside her shifted and dipped, followed by the subtle scent of expensive cologne and warm skin.

"How have you been?" Darrin asked, his voice low.

"Fine."

"How's Trevor? Has he been okay after what happened?"

The obvious concern in his voice warmed her blood and softened her just a little. "Yes and no. He's been a little clingy, which isn't his usual MO."

"I would imagine not. He seems like a pretty independent kid."

"He is. Usually. I think it just shook him up a little bit, and definitely scared him. He hasn't been wanting to go to school, which has resulted in some battles that would make Maximus Meridius proud."

"I take it you haven't been entertained?"

Her lips twitched as she fought the laughter that wanted to escape. Darrin lowered his voice to a deep baritone and said, "Are you not entertained?"

Unable to hold it any longer, she let the laughter escape.

"Oh, it's been entertaining at times. Mostly, though, I've just wanted to rip out my hair," she said once she had her laughter under control.

"He was scared, Miranda, and my guess is that he's probably embarrassed, too. We males—even those of us who are only eight years old—don't deal well with being embarrassed, especially in front of other males."

She sighed. "I know. Hell, I would have been embarrassed

too, if I'd peed my pants in front of other people at that age. I just wish I knew what to do to help."

He nudged her shoulder with his. "Just keep doing what you do. You're a great mom and you and Trevor have an amazing relationship. If he wants to talk about it, he will eventually."

"Or he'll make up some crazy story about it all."

"Or that, too, which is probably his way of processing things."

She looked at him out of the corner of her eye. "How is it that a confirmed bachelor seems to know so much about children's psychology?"

He shrugged. "Well, I was a kid once, y'know."

"You mean you didn't come out fully grown wearing a three-piece suit?"

"Uh, no." He hesitated for a few seconds, then said, "Honestly, part of it comes from experience. I was the oldest of four kids, and after our mom left Dad ended up working two, sometimes three jobs, to make sure the bills got paid and we had food on the table. So I ended up basically raising my sisters by default."

"I'm sorry."

"Shit happens."

"That's a lot of shit to put on a kid's shoulders."

"It is what it is. I was a pretty mature kid for my age, and luckily my sisters were easy to babysit. Well, except for that one time they decided to paint my nails after I'd accidentally fallen asleep."

She snorted. "It sounds like despite everything, you still love them."

"Oh, absolutely. They're all married with kids now, and being an uncle is much better than I'd thought it would be."

"You spoil them rotten, I'll bet." A smiled played at her lips.

"I try not to, but I can't always help myself. I don't know, I guess I just don't want them to go without the way we did growing up. Not that their parents don't provide for them, because they do. Somehow we've all managed to rise above our childhoods and make good lives for ourselves—and my sisters all married really good men—but I just want to give them the stuff their parents can't or won't give them. I don't want them to feel different or singled out at school, because let me tell you, it's not much fun."

Before she could even formulate a response, much less say anything, Darrin's phone vibrated. He looked down at the screen and back and her, a sheepish grin on his face. "Sorry, but I've gotta take this."

"No worries," she said as he got up and walked out of the waiting room and into the hall.

She tried to turn her attention back to the book she'd been reading, but instead found that her thoughts were focused solely on what Darrin had told her. Still waters most definitely seemed to run deep in his case.

CHAPTER TWELVE

What's your group of friends like?

A SHORT WHILE LATER A NURSE CAME INTO THE WAITING ROOM AND took Chase and Jo back to pre-op. Hugs and kisses and pats on the back were once again exchanged, and once they were out of the waiting room Sarah blew out a loud breath. Her shoulders fell slightly, and Bo grabbed his wife's hand and gave her a loving smile.

"It'll be okay, sweetheart."

Sarah nodded and blinked rapidly. "I know. I know. It's just a lot for a mama's heart to take."

"It's a happy day, okay?"

Sarah gave her husband some serious side eye and Miranda barely managed to choke back a laugh. Yes, it was a happy day, but those were still Sarah's babies back in pre-op.

It was both the blessing and the curse of being a mother.

Their conversation was interrupted by a short, elderly black woman with close-cropped hair and a friendly smile.

"Are y'all the Roberts family?"

"We are," Bo said.

"I'm Liza and I'll be your patient liaison today. Basically, I'll keep you all updated throughout the day on what's going on. I've already talked to Jo and Jenn and gotten their contact information, but wanted to let you all know that you can take turns going back to visit if you wish. Just try to keep it to two at a time. Would you like me to show you the way?"

"Yes, please," Sarah said, standing, She and Bo followed Liza out of the waiting room, leaving Owen, Caridad, Darrin, and Miranda by themselves.

Feeling awkward and out of place, Miranda went back to her book as the other three chatted.

Five minutes later it was obvious she wasn't going to be able to focus on her book. Not with Darrin so close and not with her feeling so out of place. She set the device aside and stood up. "I'm going to go find something to drink. Anyone want anything?"

"I'll take some water," Caridad said.

"Same here," said Owen, who reached into his back pocket and pulled out a wallet.

Miranda waved him off. "I've got this."

Knowing better than to argue, he replaced his wallet.

Miranda asked, "Darrin? You need anything?"

"I'm good. Thanks."

She nodded and exited the waiting room before going in search of a vending machine. Hopefully it was halfway across the building—if not in a different one all together—to give her some time to just breathe.

So of course there were vending machines literally across the hall.

Before getting everyone's drinks, though, she made use of the facilities, more to give her some breathing room than because she actually needed to.

She washed her hands and left the restroom, then stood in front of the vending machines. She fed dollar bills into one as she made her selections.

Three bottles of water, coming right up.

Curious, she peeked around the corner and saw there was yet another waiting area. This one was completely open with televisions, chairs, a couch, and numerous tables. The furniture was arranged into groupings, with shelves or half-wall dividers here and there to create slightly separated areas.

In the far corner a young woman with a baby paced, the baby in a sling against her chest and a phone to her ear. She rubbed the baby's back absently, clearly more focused on the person on the other end of the line.

A middle-aged couple sat at a bar height table, their hands clasped and heads bowed in prayer.

The bottles of water felt cold and heavy in her hands, and she felt even more out of place than she already had.

These people were all clearly in distress, connected to others in a way she could only imagine.

She turned and bumped into a hard masculine body.

Her hormones knew who it was before she'd even looked up.

Darrin wrapped his hands around her upper arms, steadying her. "I'm sorry. I didn't mean to just run into you like that."

"It's okay." She swallowed as her gaze met his. God, his eyes were beautiful.

"Liza just came and told us we could all go back to pre-op if we wanted to. They're apparently not very busy right now, so they're loosening the rules a little bit."

"Are they loosening the rules because they're not busy or because of who Matt is?" she asked dryly.

Darrin grinned, making her belly flutter. "They're saying the former but my money's on the latter."

"I guess let me go get my stuff."

"No need. Cari grabbed it and told me to find you and take you back."

"I'm sure she did." Miranda's tone was dry as they began walking towards a set of double doors on the other side of the open waiting room.

Darrin hit a button on the wall and the doors swung open. They stepped into the pre-op area and immediately heard Matt's voice followed by laughter.

Anesthesia obviously had not been administered yet.

Darrin and Miranda followed the sound of Matt's voice back to a curtained-off corner of the pre-op area. Chase and Matt were both in hospital gowns, lying in beds next to one another. The curtain that usually would have served as a divider was pulled all the way back, essentially creating one large holding area for the brothers.

"There y'all are!" Matt exclaimed quite jovially for someone who was about to have surgery.

As Miranda handed Caridad and Owen their bottles of water, Jenn said, "I really wish I was recording this right now."

"Why is that?" Darrin asked.

"Because my husband is a goofball."

Just then a woman in green scrubs approached and asked, "Alright, which one of you is Matt?"

Matt raised his hand. "That would be me."

"Alright, Mr. Roberts, I'm—wait, are you the Matt Roberts?"

"The one and only," he said with a wink. Jenn lightly smacked his bicep.

"Well, my day just got a whole lot more interesting. That was a great Game Seven, by the way," she said before glancing back down at Matt's chart. "At any rate, I'm Emma and I'll be your anesthesiologist today. You ready to get this show on the road?"

"Absolutely. Let's do this thing."

"First, I'm just going to give you an initial push through your IV. By the time we get back to the OR you should be completely passed out." Emma set a small kidney-shaped container down on a tray and picked up a syringe before sidling over to the side of Matt's bed and connecting the syringe to the IV in his hand. "Alright, Mr. Roberts, you'll probably feel a little push of fluid, and then you'll start to relax."

As she was finishing up, a couple more people showed up and introduced themselves. "How're you feeling, Mr. Roberts?" Emma asked.

"Getting a little sleepy."

"That's what we want," Emma said with a smile. "Now, tell your beautiful wife that you love her so we can roll you on back."

Matt's head lolled to the side, a goofy, love-sick grin on his face. "I love you, baby."

Jenn brushed a hand over his head and blew him a kiss. "Love you, too. I would lean over and kiss you, but bending's kind of difficult right now."

Matt rubbed her belly and slurred, "Love you too, Jelly-bean."

And then he let out a light snore and was quiet.

"Is there any way I could get some of that stuff to give him at home from time to time?" Jenn joked.

"Believe it or not, you are not the first wife to ask that," Emma said as they began to pull Matt's bed away from the wall. "We'll take good care of him, Mrs. Roberts—even if he wasn't Matt Roberts, we'd still treat him like a king."

"I know," Jenn said, completely calm.

Miranda wasn't sure how she was doing it.

And then Matt was gone. Chase still looked completely relaxed, whereas Jo looked like she was about to have a nervous breakdown. Miranda couldn't say that she blamed her.

Conversation had just started up again when a nurse came by, a white paper pill cup in one hand and a small paper cup of water in the other.

"Alright, Mr. Roberts, can you verify your name and date of birth for me?"

Chase gave her the required information.

"What I have here is your first round of anti-rejection meds. We're giving you twenty milligrams of Prednisone, ten of Prograf, and ten of Myfortic. Your maintenance doses won't be this high, we just like to give you a huge dose right before transplant."

Chase sat up and took the two cups from the nurse, said, "Well, here goes nothing," and tossed back the pills followed by a sip of water.

The nurse took both cups back from him and said, "The anesthesiologist should be by in a little bit to give you a quick exam, and once we have word that they've begun to operate on your brother we'll start getting you prepped for the OR."

She gathered up the cups and left, and all eyes turned towards Chase.

"Shit just got real," Jo whispered, her voice breaking.

Chase reached up and brushed away a tear. "Don't cry, Counselor, it's a good thing."

Jo nodded and swiped at her cheeks. "I know. It's just… heavy."

Miranda rubbed at the goosebumps that had popped up on her arms and looked away. It was impossible not to be affected, and seeing Jo trying so hard to hold herself together was a little like a punch to the gut.

Sarah sniffled.

"Don't cry, Mom."

"I gave birth to you, Chase Roberts, and I'll cry if I damned well want to," she said, echoing her earlier words with tear-strained sass.

Miranda kind of wanted to be Sarah Roberts when she grew up.

"Fair enough," Chase said.

The next thirty or so minutes flew by with constant interruptions, questions, laughter, and Jenn's cell ringing at one point. After she'd hung up, she announced, "They just started operating about five minutes ago. Looks like you're up next."

Before Chase could even formulate a response they were interrupted by a different anesthesiologist who gave him the same spiel—and happy juice—Emma had given Matt.

As they prepared to wheel Chase back to the OR Jo leaned over, kissed her husband, and said, "I love you, Cowboy."

"Love you too, Counselor," he slurred.

They wheeled him away and Jo exhaled, the sound carrying all of the weight she must have been holding on her shoulders.

Jenn stood and rubbed her best friend's back, and then silently their small group gathered up their things and walked towards the waiting area they'd previously been in.

No sooner had Jo set down her stuff than Sarah was opening her arms and wrapping Jo up in a tight embrace. Jo sobbed on Sarah's shoulder for a few minutes before visibly pulling herself back together and stepping away.

Swiping at her eyes, she said, "Sorry, y'all. The past few months have just been a bit of an emotional rollercoaster."

"You have absolutely nothing to apologize for," Sarah reassured her daughter-in-law.

"I know. I just feel like a wreck right now. A happy wreck, but a wreck nonetheless."

"Well, yeah. Your husband has kidney disease and has been rapidly deteriorating right before our very eyes," Jenn said.

"You think?" Jo asked.

"Yup. I also think all of us could probably use some food considering it's after noon and judging by the way your eyes look you have a pretty good headache."

Jo smiled. "Can't I just have wine instead?"

"Tonight, my friend. You can get drunk tonight," Jenn teased. "In the meantime, food."

They followed the signs down to the Truett Cafeteria, which was the one closest to where they were. Miranda silently followed along, grabbing a tray and plasticware before walking into the cafeteria itself.

She looked around, saw a familiar red and white logo and made a beeline for Chik-fil-a.

She and Caridad were the first to pay, so they found a large table in a quiet area.

They sat, and both women let out long sighs before looking at each other and laughing.

"I'm not the only one who feels like an outsider, right?" Miranda asked.

"Not at all. I mean, it's kind of cool to be included, but I don't quite feel like I belong."

"Same here. It's nice and all, but, yeah…"

"Yeah," Caridad echoed before taking a bite of her pizza.

Miranda followed suit, burying her discomfort in waffle fries and Polynesian sauce.

CHAPTER THIRTEEN

Why are you a good catch?

AFTER A VERY LONG DAY AT THE HOSPITAL, EVERYONE BUT BO
and Sarah gathered back at Matt and Jenn's place. Chase was
sound asleep in ICU for the night, with a kidney the transplant surgeon had proclaimed, "was peeing like a champ."
Matt was passed out in his room on the kidney and liv-
er transplant floor in Roberts, which everyone was getting a bit of a kick out of now that everything was done.

Jo and Jenn had visited both men, reassured themselves
their husbands were fine, and had finally been dragged away
from the hospital by Owen.

Per Jenn's promise earlier, Darrin had stopped by Spec's
on the way back to Matt's house and picked up several bottles
of wine and a few six packs of beer. He'd also picked up some
lime and sangria-flavored Topo Chico for Jenn, considering
she couldn't join them in the alcohol consumption.

Darrin set his box of booze on the kitchen island and began taking things out, refrigerating as necessary.

Jenn walked in, wearing plaid pajama pants and a tank top
that stretched tightly across her rounded belly. Even after a
long day at the hospital she still glowed.

Her eyes lit up when she saw him lift two glass bottles

of lime Topo Chico out of the box. "Oh, if I wasn't married I could kiss you right now."

Darrin laughed and offered her one of the bottles. "I really don't want Matt trying to kick my ass when he wakes up in the morning."

"I think he might understand in this case," she said as she retrieved a bottle opener from a drawer.

"Where's everyone else?" he asked as he placed a six pack in the fridge.

"Out on the patio. I'd just happened to be coming in for some water anyway."

Darrin grabbed a beer for himself before closing the refrigerator. He picked up the bottle opener Jenn had set on the island and popped off the cap before leaning back against the countertop.

"How're you holding up?" he asked.

Jenn sighed and pulled out a chair so she could sit. "Okay. Better than I thought I would, honestly, but I also can't really afford to let nerves and anxiety get the best of me, either."

She absently rubbed her belly, making him smile.

"No, I supposed you can't. Besides, he's a stubborn SOB. He'll be okay."

She laughed. "He's so stubborn. Thank God, otherwise I don't know that we would even be speaking right now, much less married."

He looked down at the beer bottle in his hand before looking back up at Jenn. "Honestly? I think you two would have eventually ended up together no matter what. It wasn't really a matter of 'if,' so much as 'when.'"

She cocked her head to the side. "You knew more than you let on," she said, referring to the previous summer when she and Matt had gotten together.

"I knew enough. I knew about San Antonio. I knew he'd been hung up on you ever since then. The only thing I didn't know until last summer was your name. Up until then I'd just called you San Antonio Girl."

Jenn snorted. "That sounds like a really bad country song. San Antonio Girl."

"Truth." He smiled. "Honestly, though? I'm glad you decided to give him a second chance. It's nice seeing him happy, and you're obviously good for him."

"What about you?"

His fingers flexed around the beer bottle. "What about me?"

She peered at him over the top of her mineral water. "Any thoughts of finding someone and settling down?"

"Not a chance." He pushed away from the counter. "In case you haven't noticed, my lifestyle and career aren't exactly conducive to long-term relationships, much less families."

Jenn slowly got up before following him to the patio doors. "Excuses, excuses. If you wanted to make it work, you could."

Instead of responding he turned the knob on one of the French doors and held it open for her. She walked through—Topo Chico still firmly in hand—before taking a seat next to Jo.

He probably wouldn't admit it to anyone, but he loved Matt and Jenn's patio area. Or "outdoor living space" as their Realtor had called it.

The flagstone patio itself was probably twenty by twenty, and fully covered. A large ceiling fan hung from the structure and lazily oscillated, stirring the air and helping to keep away mosquitoes. In one corner was a large, flat-screen television with what would normally be a fully stocked bar underneath it. On the opposite side was an outdoor kitchen, complete with mammoth smoker and grill, mini fridge, and sink. Comfortable chairs and chaise lounges, along with a low table, completed the area, which was lit with strung-up lights that reminded him of bulbs from days gone by.

He could live out here if he didn't think he would totally be in Matt and Jenn's way.

The only remaining open seat was next to Miranda, which

he took as a sign from above.

Or at the very least, a golden opportunity.

She was deep in conversation with Caridad, though, so instead of saying anything he decided to listen in and try to figure out what made her tick.

As he listened to the two women, one thing became clear to him—if he wanted Miranda, he was going to have to work for it.

The idea was admittedly a bit foreign to him. Not that he hadn't had to put in some effort before with women, it was just that, well, he usually didn't have to put in a lot of effort.

With Miranda, though, he suspected that his usual tactics of wooing a woman wouldn't work. Even without knowing her as well as he would like to, he knew her well enough to realize that she wasn't the type to be impressed—or swayed—by candlelit dinners or fussy bouquets.

No, the way to Miranda's heart was through the things she cared about—Trevor, wildlife, and maybe even astronomy. And since even he wasn't cut-throat enough to try to use her son in order to get to her, he was going to have to go with either plan B or C.

She laughed at something Caridad said, and he was unable to hold back a smile. He may be above leveraging Trevor—but he had no problem drafting Caridad to his cause if necessary.

CHAPTER FOURTEEN

What are your best qualities?

MIRANDA WALKED FROM THE BARN TO THE HOUSE, EXHAUSTION weighing down her feet. It had been a long day of manual labor—filling wildlife waterers, lifting bags of feed, and planting food plots. Not to mention getting up early to take Trevor into town so he could spend the weekend with her parents.

Sure, if she'd still been working for Texas Parks & Wildlife, days like these wouldn't really happen, but she wouldn't change her job for the world.

Speaking of her job…she looked up as she neared the house and saw a familiar car parked in the driveway. Resignation and excitement warred in her head, making her frown.

Well, there went her plans for a night in alone, vegging in front of the TV while watching movies on Netflix she couldn't usually watch when Trevor was home.

Steeling herself—and grimacing at her appearance—she opened the door to the kitchen and stepped inside.

Two things hit her at once—one, her unfortunate attraction to him had not gone away in the past few weeks since the transplant, and two…he looked to be cooking supper.

His back was to her, so she took a couple of seconds to look her fill and praise God for khaki shorts. Sure, Wranglers and baseball pants were on top of the Mount Rushmore of God's gifts to women, but in her opinion khaki shorts definitely deserved some consideration.

He still hadn't noticed her, so she allowed her gaze to travel over the rest of his body. Muscular calves that spoke of his life as a former athlete who kept himself in shape. Bare feet. And then back up to, well, the main event, followed by a soft-looking t-shirt that stretched across his shoulders. The pink should have looked feminine, but instead all it did was highlight his gorgeous skin tone.

He stood at the stove, stirring something in a pot. It smelled heavenly.

She must have made some sort of noise, because he suddenly looked over his shoulder and totally caught her looking.

He smiled and her cheeks flamed.

So much for acting unaffected.

Deciding there was nothing to do other than face the man in what surprisingly looked to be his natural habitat, she walked over to the island and pulled out a stool.

"Forgive me if this sounds rude, but what are you doing here?"

He turned down the heat on the stove before walking over to the refrigerator. After taking something out of it, he sauntered over to the island and slid a beer in front of her. Warily, she twisted off the cap before taking a long pull.

"I wanted to see you."

She almost spit out her beer.

"Why?"

He smiled that devastating smile, and she was glad she was sitting down.

"Because I like you."

She blinked rapidly, then asked again, "Why?"

He chuckled. "Because you're interesting. Intelligent. Beautiful."

She stared at the dirt lodged under her fingernails.

"I like smart women, and I really like a sense of humor.

You definitely have both of those qualities."

"Yeah, but I've also been pretty up-front with you, Darrin. I'm not looking for a relationship and I'm certainly not interested in a hook-up." She looked up and met his gaze head-on, somehow managing to not go up in flames from the heat in it. "And I'm sure as hell not interested in sleeping with my boss."

"I'm not your boss; Owen and Chase are."

She rolled her eyes. "Semantics. We've been over this before. You're an owner, therefore my employer. That's an ethical line I'm not willing to cross."

"What if I wasn't an owner?"

"Excuse me?"

He repeated his question.

"You're freaking crazy."

He raised an eyebrow. "Am I, though? I know next to nothing about hunting or wildlife management. I live up in Dallas, and I hadn't even been here until this year. It's not like I'm an active owner or anything."

"But the investment..."

He shrugged.

"You would seriously give up your ownership stake to score points with me?"

"I wouldn't quite put it that way."

She pushed away her beer and stood. "Then how would you put it, Darrin? Because from where I'm standing it sounds like you think that all it would take to get in my pants is to no longer be an owner of the Devils Ranch, which quite frankly sounds a lot like a really bad Lifetime movie."

She turned and began to walk away.

"I didn't mean to insult you."

She breathed deeply, searching for calm. Instead of finding it, though, she just found anger. "You know what, Darrin? Go fuck yourself."

She left the room to nothing but the sound of silence.

Well that hadn't gone as he'd expected.

Darrin watched Miranda's retreating form and tried to figure out how that had gone so poorly.

Well, to be fair, he wasn't so dim that he didn't realize how his question could have come across as a bit high-handed and presumptive.

On the flip-side of that, she hadn't exactly stuck around to hear him out, either.

He sighed and went back to the marinara he'd been stirring when she'd walked in. Hopefully he could get back into her good graces with portobello-stuffed ravioli, salad, and garlic bread. If not, well….he'd figure something out.

After taking a shower and changing into clean clothes, Miranda snuck out the back door and made her way over to Daniel's apartment, which was basically a barn loft that had been converted to a living space.

Sure, sneaking out was a bit childish, but she just couldn't deal with Darrin anymore right now.

The man made her feel a screwed up combination of angry and horny—not exactly a healthy combo.

Not that running to Daniel was necessarily healthy, either, but he'd already invited her over for dinner prior to that… whatever it was…thing that had happened with Darrin.

Still feeling pissed and insulted, she rapped sharply on Daniel's door, which swung open almost immediately.

He'd also changed clothes, and was now wearing cargo shorts and a Devils Ranch t-shirt. He smiled at her, and she wondered—not for the first time—why she wasn't attracted to him. Sure, he was a few years younger than she was, but he was also intelligent, hard-working, and hot as hell.

If she had to be attracted to someone, why couldn't it be Daniel rather than Darrin? Sure, dating Daniel could get a little complicated—especially if things went south—but it couldn't get anywhere near as complicated as getting involved with Darrin would be.

"Hey. Glad you could make it," Daniel said before stepping aside and gesturing for her to come in.

She entered his apartment and he closed the door behind her.

"You want a beer or anything?"

She snorted. "Tequila sounds like a much better option right about now."

He raised a dark eyebrow. "Tequila? What the hell happened between us calling it a day and you showing up here?"

She flopped onto his couch, which was this huge, fluffy monstrosity that looked like it had been through a tornado or two. It was also the most comfortable couch ever.

"I just…had an unpleasant conversation is all." She wasn't about to get into a discussion with Daniel about Darrin.

There'd been enough awkward today, thankyouverymuch.

"Okay then." A bottle of Patron and a shot glass appeared in front of her face. She grabbed both and set them on the coffee table in front of her. "Give me a second and I'll get some limes. You want anything to eat before you dive into that? I haven't started supper yet, so…"

She took the top off the tequila and splashed some into the shot glass. "You got the stuff to make nachos? That sounds good right now."

"Nachos and tequila. That must have been one hell of a conversation."

She didn't wait for salt or lime and knocked back the shot.

"You have no idea," she mumbled before setting the shot glass back on the coffee table.

She stared at the liquor, her mind wandering back to that conversation with Darrin. Of all the asinine things he could have said, intimating that she would sleep with him if he wasn't an owner of the ranch was at the top of the list.

Not that he wasn't partially right, it was just the way he'd said it, like she was some kind of whore or something. Well, she had news for him—she wasn't the type of woman who could easily be bought. Nor was she the type of woman to fall at a guy's feet just because he had a killer smile, more money than God, and an ass worthy of having sonnets written about it.

Nope.

She so wasn't that type of woman.

But damn did he have a nice smile.

And, okay, so he was a good kisser, too. Great, if she was being honest with herself. But she wasn't interested in Darrin's kisses or his smile or his ass.

Not when those things came with an attitude that made her feel like she was as easy to buy as a politician.

And that so was not the case.

The couch dipping beside her jolted her out of her thoughts, making her shake her head slightly to clear it.

"Those must've been some pretty deep thoughts you were having just then."

She shrugged a shoulder and grabbed a nacho off the plate he'd set on the coffee table, but didn't say anything.

Daniel sighed and grabbed a nacho of his own.

They ate in companionable silence, and once again Miranda wondered why she wasn't attracted to him. They got along great when he wasn't making ill-timed declarations of love, which admittedly had only happened that one time. But still. That one time had been more than enough.

The fact remained, though, that she liked Daniel. She just didn't want to get naked with Daniel.

And therein laid the problem.

Without saying a word, he handed her a lime wedge and salt shaker before pouring two shots of tequila. In tandem, they licked the salt, took the shot, then sucked on their limes. They did that a few more times, until Miranda was feeling pleasantly fuzzy-headed and slightly more relaxed than she had been.

Logically, she knew alcohol was not the answer, but it also wasn't as if she did this on a regular basis, either. Hell, the last time she'd been drunk was the night she'd gotten pregnant with Trevor.

She thunked her head back on the couch.

Oh, God, she really was a cliche, wasn't she?

"You ready to talk about it yet?" Daniel asked.

She rolled her head and looked at him. "I'm a cliche of a woman, Daniel."

"What?"

"I'm a cliche of a woman."

"How so?"

She held up a finger with each statement. "One, I got pregnant while having drunk sex. Two, the baby daddy just walked out without saying a word once he found out I was pregnant. Three, I'm the lonely single mom romance novels get written about. Four, I have the hots for a man who's probably a millionaire, which is another cliche all on its own. Five, that man is technically my boss. Six, my guy friend has a crush on me that I've never reciprocated. Seven, I'm getting drunk to stop thinking but it isn't working. Eight, I forgot that tequila makes my clothes fall off."

She clapped her hands over her mouth on that last one as Daniel's eyes widened. His gaze briefly dropped down to her chest and then back up to her face, and a slight pink tinged his cheeks.

"I did not just say that."

"I think you did."

"I think that might have been a little mean of me."

He snorted. "Nah."

She leaned over and—against her better judgment—poured herself another shot. Daniel tried to take it from her, but she downed it just as his hand wrapped around hers. She tightened her hold on the glass and licked her lips, then made what was probably one of the worst decisions of her life.

She leaned in and kissed him.

Daniel, bless his heart, kissed her back, albeit nowhere near as enthusiastically as she'd figured he would have. And she'd give him credit—he was a really good kisser—but other than a sort of detached curiosity she felt...nothing.

Feeling like a balloon that had suddenly lost all its air, she pulled away and wilted into the couch cushions. Eyes closed, she licked her lips then said, "I'm sorry, Daniel. I shouldn't have done that."

"No, it's okay." He sounded confused, which made her open one eye so she could look at him.

"Am I that bad of a kisser?"

He shook his head. "No. Not at all. You're a great kisser. I just...that wasn't what I'd expected."

Too embarrassed to say anything, she closed her eye again and waited him out.

"I mean...I really don't know how to say this without it sounding bad...but I'd expected to feel more."

Oh, God, kill her now.

"And I think that came out wrong." He drew in a ragged breath. "What I mean is that I'd had this crush on you and was convinced you were the perfect woman. I've thought about kissing you and, well, let's not get into that because this is getting really embarrassing. I just expected to feel more, is all."

Even though her cheeks felt like they were on fire and her stomach felt like it could stage a revolt that would make the Boston Tea Party proud, she opened her eyes and really looked at Daniel.

He appeared to be just as embarrassed as she was, which made her feel marginally better, so she girded her loins and asked, "Are you saying you didn't feel anything?"

"Other than a pleasant kiss? Nada."

She breathed a sigh of relief. "Me either. Zilch. I mean, you're a good kisser and it was pleasant and all it's just... yeah."

He relaxed into the couch cushions and turned his head to look at her. "Yeah."

And then they both promptly burst into laughter.

CHAPTER FIFTEEN

What types of activities do you like to do with someone you're dating?

DARRIN WAS SITTING IN A CHAIR ON THE PATIO, GOING THROUGH email on his iPad, when he noticed the beam of a flashlight bobbing up and down, making its way towards the house. Glancing at the time on his watch, he saw it was just after midnight and frowned before looking in the direction the light was coming from.

If he wasn't mistaken, Daniel's apartment was a converted loft in that particular barn. Maybe the ranch foreman had decided to come over to the main house for something.

He was just about to sit down when the light made a sudden turn and started moving more towards him. As it drew closer, he was able to make out the features of the person holding the flashlight.

It wasn't Daniel.

He schooled his face to hide his surprise that Miranda had just left the ranch foreman's apartment, and remained silent as she shuffled towards him. Wordlessly, she sat in the chair next to his and turned off her flashlight. He thought he caught the faint whiff of tequila, and felt twin daggers of jealousy and self-hatred.

Jealousy that she'd apparently chosen to go drink with Daniel rather than have dinner with him, and self-hatred that he'd bungled their conversation so badly that he'd driven her away.

"I realize I probably shouldn't have snuck out, especially when you were obviously cooking dinner, but you really, really pissed me off."

She sounded sober, but he had to wonder if that was an illusion considering A, the tequila scent and B, the fact that she wasn't usually quite so direct with him.

"I should have framed my question better."

She stood and began to pace. "It's not just that, Darrin. Yeah, your question was worded poorly, but it's everything. I feel like you're not listening to me, like you're so used to getting what you want that you can't even fathom that maybe you don't always get what you want. I feel like you're just trying to barge your way in without even knocking on the door, and where I come from that can get you shot in the most literal sense of the word. But it's like I keep talking, I keep telling you to back off, and you won't take no for answer. And then for you to just assume that my only reason for telling you no is because you're an owner of the ranch? That's pretty pompous, if you ask me, and doesn't necessarily paint you in the best light."

Her words hit him like hail on a windshield, bouncing off after leaving a mark.

She whirled around and faced him, her blonde hair swirling around her shoulders and her hands on her hips. "Here's the thing, Darrin. I think you're far too hot for your own good. Yes, I'm physically attracted to you, but I have a whole hell of a lot more to consider than myself and a few orgasms. Beyond that, yes, you're intelligent and successful and on paper I can totally see why you were named Dallas' Most Eligible Bachelor. My guess is that you're used to women who just fall at your feet."

"I hate that I'm attracted to you."

She looked away, unable to continue to meet his gaze. It was too intense. Too knowing.

She felt like it was cutting right through her.

He wouldn't let her look away, though, wouldn't let her hide, and he stood up and stepped towards her before gently cupping her cheek and turning her head so that they were looking at each other.

"I didn't necessarily ask to be attracted to you, either, but I am."

A frustrated growl vibrated in the back of her throat. "You're not the one who has everything to lose, though, Darrin. You're not the one who has more than yourself to think about. For you, this is simple. It's easy. For me, though, it's not. It's not easy or simple at all."

"You don't think I get that?" He ran a hand over his face. "I screwed up earlier with that question, and I knew it as soon as the words left my mouth. But then you ran off and didn't even give me a chance to explain or apologize."

"So now I'm the bad guy?"

"No one's the bad guy here. That's not what I'm saying."

She took a deep breath, trying to calm herself down. It wasn't easy, considering she felt like she was caught in the middle of a hurricane after drinking a case of Red Bull followed by an espresso chaser.

And wow, she'd totally just mixed her metaphors.

"Miranda, I know that you have more than yourself to think about, and if you weren't taking Trevor into consideration I don't know that I would like you as much as I do. I know I sure as hell wouldn't respect you as much as I do. But you're more than your son. You're more than a mom. You're a beautiful, intelligent, vibrant woman who's been driving me absolutely crazy since I first laid eyes on you, and that's not something I'm used to."

She snorted, trying to hold on to the anger that was slowly seeping out of her. "Yeah, right. You and I both know that you could pretty much have any woman you wanted with barely batting an eyelash. I'm only driving you crazy because I'm not easy."

"That's probably part of it."

"Well, at least you admit it."

"I try to be honest, and I'm not going to insult your intelligence and stand here and tell you that I'm not intrigued and weirdly excited by the thought of really having to put in the effort with you."

"Wow, that made you sound like a cocky asshole."

"Yeah, I know. I'm not necessarily proud of that, either."

And he wasn't, she could see that written clearly across his face.

The magnetic pull she felt whenever he was around threatened to pull her in, pull her under. As she stared into his eyes, she felt almost hypnotized, and her body swayed towards his of its own volition. What would it be like to just let go? To forget—just for a little while—all the things that kept her so buttoned up and untouchable?

His thumb brushed her cheek, the movement soothing and yet arousing.

Her body swayed closer to his, until there was barely a breath of air between them. His thumb moved from her cheek to her mouth, over her bottom lip, making her skin feel like sparks danced wherever he touched.

"I hate that I'm so attracted to you," she repeated, her voice a whisper.

"I know," he whispered back.

And then she threw caution to the wind and pressed her lips to his; if she ended up regretting this in the morning, she would deal with it then.

For tonight, she just wanted to feel.

The feel of Miranda's lips against his was quite possibly the best thing he'd felt in years. Or at least since the last time he'd kissed her.

She tasted like tequila and lime, a heady combination that hit him with the force of a freight train.

He had a brief moment of hesitation—she'd been drinking, and no matter how badly he wanted her he wasn't about to take advantage of her in an inebriated state—but then she pressed her body completely against his and wrapped her arms around his neck, and his brain kind of short-circuited.

Her hands pressed into the base of his skull, pressing him closer. His hands moved to wrap around her hips, pulling her body completely flush against his. She released a breathy little moan, and he grew even harder than he already was.

It wasn't a gentle kiss. It was full of lips and tongues and teeth. It was kind of angry.

It was the hottest damned kiss he'd ever had.

She pressed harder against him, her stomach rubbing against his erection. His fingers dug into her ass, pulling her even closer before picking her up. She wrapped her legs around his waist, and he somehow managed to make it to his room without dropping her or running them into any furniture or walls.

He kicked the door closed behind them, then took the few short steps to the bed, where he lowered them without breaking contact.

Her hips undulated under his, her center pressing and rubbing against his cock in a move that almost had him coming in his pants.

Her hands slid under his t-shirt, and then under the waistband of his shorts and boxer briefs, making him flex involuntarily.

A part of his brain was screaming at him to slow things down, to take his time so that he could commit every detail to memory.

The other part was urging him to rip off her clothes and

bury himself inside of her as soon as possible.

One of her hands circled around and grasped his cock, and all thoughts of taking his time flew out the window.

She knew it had been a long time since she'd had a dick in her hand, but she didn't remember Trevor's dad's being quite so...impressive.

Which almost made her giggle, because hello, stereotypes.

She wasn't complaining, though.

And then all thoughts of giggling and comparing fled when Darrin literally tore off her tank top. Just ripped the fabric, right down the middle.

Before she could even think of an appropriate response he'd pushed the cups of her bra down and plumped her breasts up before sucking a nipple into his mouth.

Oh sweet, heavenly Jesus.

His teeth grazed the tip, nipping lightly, and she went a little crazy, pushing his shorts and underwear down while he unbuttoned her jeans and pushed them and her panties down to her ankles. She kicked them off and fused her lips to his again. He broke the kiss briefly, leaned down and grabbed his wallet from his shorts pocket and pulled out a string of condoms.

"Feeling lucky, were you?" she teased.

"Hopeful," he said before separating one foil packet from the rest, ripping it open and rolling the latex down his shaft. She hooked her legs around his hips, pulling him closer, needing him inside of her.

Instead of complying though, he suddenly decided to slow things down. He glided long fingers over her stomach, causing goosebumps to scatter. Through the curls at the juncture of her thighs until they parted her. One finger circled around her entrance while another played with her clit, making her gasp and arch towards him.

"Why'd you slow down?" she panted.

He chuckled. "To make sure you were ready."

She arched her hips again as he slid a finger inside of her. She moaned. "I think I'm good to go."

His only response was to lower his head and wrap his lips around a turgid nipple before drawing his finger out of her before pushing it back in. His mouth played with her breasts as he finger fucked her, his thumb applying just enough pressure to her clit to get her close but not push her over the edge. Her hips moved in time with his hand. Her breath caught when he added a second finger to the mix, stretching her and filling her more completely.

Tension gathered in her belly and the base of her spine, swirling, causing her muscles to tense and goosebumps to scatter across her entire body.

Darrin's fingers pumped faster, harder, making her body fly higher and higher until she shattered into a million pieces, her body convulsing around him as she gasped for air.

He removed his fingers and she had a brief moment of feeling empty, but then he slammed his cock into her and she'd never felt so full—so complete—in her life.

Darrin ground his hips against hers and wound his fingers through her hair. The sensation should have hurt, but instead it just turned her on even more as her pussy continued to pulse and contract from the orgasm he'd given her.

His pace was relentless. She dug her fingers into his ass—God, that delectable, amazing ass—and urged him on. Higher. Harder. He was already buried to the hilt and yet she wanted him deeper, closer, touching all the places that hadn't been touched in years.

"God, I need you." His breath was hot against her neck, his words a low, possessive growl.

She felt a sudden gush of wetness, and absently realized it had come from her.

Before she could think beyond that, though, he'd pulled out and flipped her over onto her stomach. She'd never been a fan of doggy style before, but something about the way he handled her as if she wasn't fragile, as if he needed her right now or else, made her more than willing to draw up her knees and push back against him as he slammed into her from behind.

She buried her face in the comforter, stifling the moan that rocked through her body.

God, he felt even bigger than he had before, and every time he slammed into her she felt it...just...right...there.

Completely unselfconscious at this point—this was sex in its most raw, basic form—she reached between her legs and played with her clit.

"Fuck, baby, that's hot."

She moved her finger faster, his words and cock driving her higher and higher. He drove into her, again and again, filling her completely and rubbing against some magical place with every single stroke. And yet she hovered there on that precipice, needing something she couldn't name to push her over the edge.

"What do you need, baby?"

"I don't know," she managed to gasp out. "I'm so close."

His hands tightened on her hips before moving, gliding over her ass and digging in there. She moaned, then briefly stiffened when she felt a finger drift down and between her cheeks, parting the globes of her ass as he moved lower before pressing that finger against what was most definitely virgin territory.

But then he did something with his hips, making her gasp and push back in search of more where that came from, and then his finger was inside of her there and holy, "Fuuuuuu..."

Her orgasm exploded, flooding her entire body with sensation. Her feet cramped and her head got fuzzy as she convulsed around his cock. With a groan, Darrin slammed into her one last time, his fingers digging into her hips as he pushed harder, higher inside of her.

She pushed back against him, wanting it all, wanting as much as he had to give.

Wanting everything.

CHAPTER SIXTEEN

What's your idea of a relaxing weekend?

MIRANDA WOKE UP IN A BED THAT WASN'T HER OWN WITH SORE muscles and a pounding headache.

It was like a weird flashback to her college days prior to getting pregnant. Well, except for the whole strange bed thing considering she'd only ever been with one other person prior to last night.

She braced herself for the glare of sunlight before cracking open an eyelid, only to find that the shades had been drawn, the lights were out, and there was a bottle of water and a bottle of aspirin on the nightstand. Darrin's side of the bed was empty, causing relief to rush through her.

Sure, there was still the awkward morning after to be had, but at least this way she could at least brush her hair and teeth before facing it. And definitely take those aspirin.

She sat up slowly before swinging her legs over the edge of the mattress, mentally kicking herself for drinking so much tequila last night. As an undergrad she'd been able to more than hold her own, but once she'd found out she was pregnant life had most definitely changed dramatically.

Since Trevor had been born, she could count on two fingers the number of times she'd been drunk. The first was the day she'd found out Trevor's father had been killed by a road-side bomb. The second was yesterday.

The fact that both times were because of a man was not lost upon her, but her head hurt too much to laugh—or cry—about it.

She downed the aspirin and water, then got up and searched for her clothes. How her panties had ended up on top of a lampshade and her bra across the room she had no idea, but at least she'd found them.

Not that she exactly had a super long walk of shame ahead of her, but still.

She dressed slowly and as well as she could considering the state of her tank top, then cracked open the bedroom door to look out into the hallway. All clear. She turned left and hurried down to her own bedroom, only breathing a sigh of relief when the door was closed and locked behind her.

With every step she took her thigh muscles burned, and she felt swollen and tender between her legs. Despite the fact that it had been quite a while since the last time she'd been intimate with anyone other than herself, she couldn't recall Trevor's dad ever making her feel so...well-ridden...for lack of a better term.

Even alone, her cheeks flamed at the thought.

Well, to be fair, he did definitely ride you last night.

She groaned at the thought before pushing away from the door and making her way to her private bathroom, where she stripped back down before turning on the water in the walk-in shower to give it time to warm up.

She went through the motions in a bit of a daze, her thoughts rolling around in her head like west Texas tumble-weeds.

Images from the night before filtered through her mind like a slow motion replay, making her skin tingle and nipples pebble. As she remembered what it had felt like that first time he'd thrust inside, her clit throbbed and her womb clinched.

With a groan she rested her forehead against the shower

wall and slid her hand between her legs as her mind played back the events from last night. She was tender and swollen and yet still so fucking turned on she came almost immediately on a gasp, the release managing to take the edge off while making her wish Darrin was inside of her again.

Her breathing heavy and her hands at her sides, she closed her eyes and let the water pour over her, wishing it could wash away this want as easily as it did soap bubbles.

Darrin looked up from his phone as Miranda walked into the kitchen, and without a word he removed the plate he'd had warming in the oven and set it on the island. He'd had a feeling she would be hungover—with either tequila, regret, or both—this morning, so he'd prepared his favorite morning after omelet for her, along with a side of bacon and fresh strawberries that he'd found in the refrigerator.

She didn't say anything, but the fact that she chose to sit down at the island gave him hope, so he poured her a cup of coffee and doctored it just the way she liked it—with a splash of half and half and a teaspoon of sugar—and set that in front of her as well. He grabbed his own coffee and sat across from her, secretly amused. She was apparently grouchy when she had a hangover.

She picked up her fork and cut off a bite of egg, then let out a small sound of pleasure as she swallowed.

"You can cook, too?" she asked, finally breaking the silence.

He chuckled. "Too?"

She swallowed another piece of omelet before responding. "Yes, too. We've already established that you're wealthy, successful, and attractive. Adding the ability to cook to that list just seems unfair."

He cupped his hands around the coffee mug in front of him. "I've honestly never thought much about it."

"Somehow I doubt that."

"What does that mean?"

She shrugged a shoulder, and his gaze followed the motion as he remembered what her skin had felt like against his last night. He mentally shook himself and tried to focus on the conversation at hand.

"It means that you don't seem like the type of man who does anything without having a good reason to." She pointed her fork at him. "And before you go thinking that's in insult, it's not. Despite the fact that I don't know you that well, I have figured that much out. You're a planner, Darrin Mann."

"There's nothing wrong with planning."

"Never said there was."

"You're making me sound like a calculating asshole."

"I don't know that 'calculating' would be the right word. 'Opportunistic,' maybe."

"That doesn't sound much better."

She looked down at her plate and pushed the remaining eggs around with her fork. "I know, and I don't mean for it to sound so bad. I mean, yeah, you're calculating and opportunistic, but if there's one thing I learned from Jerry Maguire it's that sports agents kind of have to be a little calculating and opportunistic. Cut-throat, I think you called it once before."

"You're really basing your knowledge of my profession on a twenty-year-old movie?"

Her head shot up. "Has it seriously been twenty years? Holy shit, I wasn't even in middle school when it first came out."

"And I was in high school."

Her cheeks turned pink and she swallowed before saying, "I don't even know how old you are."

Darrin somehow managed not to laugh—barely. "Does it matter?"

"In the grand scheme of things? Probably not. I just..." she set her fork down then picked up a piece of bacon and snapped it in half. "Last night was not ordinary behavior for me, and it's kind of embarrassing to admit that at thirty years old I'm not entirely sure what the protocol is for the morning after what happened last night."

"You mean fucking each other's brains out?"

She narrowed her eyes at him, but her cheeks and chest flushed with color and he could make out the outline of her pebbled nipples pushing against the fabric of her bra and tank top.

"Yeah, I mean fucking each other's brains out."

The sound of a throat clearing had both of them turning their heads towards the sound. Daniel stood just inside the front door with a bemused expression on his face. "Sorry to interrupt what sounds like a really interesting conversation, y'all, but Miranda, we have a bit of a problem."

If her head hadn't still been dully aching she would have banged it against the island. "What now?"

"Long story short, there's a fire."

"Where?"

"Next ranch over. From what little I've been told, it's probably a good five miles away from us, but it's windy and they're calling for as much help as they can get."

She slid off her stool and headed back towards her bedroom, saying over her shoulder, "Let me put on some appropriate clothes. How big is the fire right now?"

"Almost a hundred acres."

"Shit." It was still relatively small considering they were talking about thousands of acres of land, but a hundred acres on fire could easily turn into two hundred then five hundred then a thousand on up. Especially with dry, windy conditions like they'd had the past couple of weeks.

The only saving grace, she thought as she slipped on a pair of flame resistant pants, was that they'd had a really wet spring and vegetation was incredibly green rather than being dry and brittle.

Not quite as much tinder as there would have been even

eight months ago, thankfully, but definitely still enough to pose a real threat to surrounding ranches.

She grabbed a pair of socks from her top drawer, pulled them on and then slipped her feet into a pair of boots before grabbing a hair tie off the top of her dresser. She was in the process of pulling her hair into a makeshift French braid when she bumped into Darrin in the hallway.

"What can I do to help?"

She glanced at his clothes—they were obviously designer—and back up to his face. "How much do you love those jeans?"

He shrugged. "They're just blue jeans."

"Fair enough. Come on, then, I'm sure they can use all the hands they can get."

She finished braiding her hair and wrapped the hair tie around the end a couple of times as they entered the living room. "Alright, let's go."

Daniel looked from her to Darrin, unable to disguise the surprise on his face. He quickly schooled his features, though, and hefted a YETI cooler off the floor. "I threw as much bottled water, Gatorade, and ice in here as I could."

"Good thinking. Let me grab a couple boxes of protein bars from the pantry," Miranda said before crossing over to the walk-in pantry, where she grabbed a few different boxes of protein bars, along with cheese and peanut butter crackers. Odds were they had a long day ahead of them and would need all the sustenance and hydration they could get.

The three of them moved quickly out of the house and to Daniel's pickup. He'd already hooked up a trailer with a five-hundred-gallon water tank on it, and a gas-powered water pump sat beside it, ready to go.

"You've been busy," she commented as they threw their supplies into the bed of the truck.

"I woke up and smelled smoke before I saw it. Had a feeling we might end up needing it today."

They climbed into the truck and quickly made their way

to the gate and then onto the county road. It didn't take long to figure out where the fire was—the smoke was billowing up towards the sky in a huge, puffy gray cloud and ash began to rain down on the truck.

Daniel turned into a driveway—its gate standing open—and made his way to a clearing beside the main house, where several fire trucks and other vehicles were gathered. A few volunteer firefighters were wiping sweat off their brows and chugging down water.

They got out of the truck and quickly made their way over to the gathered group. She knew most of the people there from her time with Texas Parks & Wildlife, and they all greeted her warmly despite the danger burning just a short distance away.

"So what's the status?" Daniel asked.

"We've got it about seventy percent contained right now, but it's burned at least five hundred acres already," responded one of the firefighters.

Daniel whistled through his teeth. "Livestock, people, and buildings?"

"We've got some missing cows, but luckily the fire started away from any structures."

Daniel nodded. "Just let us know what we can do. We brought some water, Gatorade, and snacks—it's not much, but we figured y'all could use it."

"Thanks, man," the firefighter said before tossing his empty water bottle into the bed of a nearby pickup truck.

"Have y'all set up fire breaks yet?" Miranda asked.

The firefighter shook his head. "Not yet. We haven't had the manpower for someone to climb on the bull dozer."

"I've had some training. I can do it."

"You've had wildfire training?" Darrin asked.

"Well, yeah. Fire is a fact of life out here and it impacts all of our wildlife and vegetation."

"Fair enough."

Someone tossed a set of keys towards her, which she caught mid-air. "Alright, boys, what's the game plan?"

CHAPTER SEVENTEEN

What's the most fun part of dating?

DARRIN WIPED YET MORE SWEAT OFF HIS BROW AND THOUGHT FOR the thousandth time that day that he had a newfound respect for firefighters. Not that he hadn't respected them before, but helping out here definitely gave one a slightly different perspective on how hard they worked to keep others safe.

The sun had set at least an hour ago, yet it seemed like they were nowhere near having this fire contained. Over the course of the day it had managed to jump breaks almost as soon as they'd been created and had expanded to just over a thousand acres.

The good news was that this particular ranch backed up to the Devils River, creating a natural fire break on one side. The bad news was that fire didn't seem to understand boundaries and had jumped the fence onto the next property over.

The good news was that it was moving away from what he'd started thinking of as command central—and thus away from the Devils Ranch on the other side. The bad news was that dozens of heads of cattle and hundreds of sheep were missing.

He handed a bottle of water to yet another sooty-faced firefighter, and somehow managed to tamp down on the feeling that he wasn't doing enough. He was used to taking charge and leading, so standing back and letting others take over felt beyond unnatural to him.

That being said, he was smart enough to realize that he knew nothing about fighting fires and that his presence out on the front lines could possibly hurt more than help.

So he'd put his skills to work here close to the ranch house, setting up a command center. Working with the owner Barry's wife—Nancy—and other people who'd shown up to help, they'd set up a couple of makeshift tents with several folding tables in the shade. Someone had made a run into Del Rio and bought a couple dozen flats of water and snacks, which they'd placed in ice chests and on tabletops. Nancy had pulled out a couple of five-gallon dispensers that she'd mixed Gatorade in and seemed to constantly be refilling. There was also a steady stream of food from neighbors dropping by, from casseroles to barbecue to sandwiches. They'd also designated one corner of the tent for first-aid for minor wounds such as blisters, splinters, cuts, and burns. Darrin had called in a helicopter pilot the ranch sometimes contracted with and offered to pay him triple his going rate if he would be willing to stay on standby in case of a medical emergency.

He'd been more than willing.

Other regional fire departments had shown up, too, with a couple of trucks coming in from Del Rio and a handful coming in from Sonora and Rocksprings. It was impressive how so many people—a lot of them complete strangers—had come together in such a short amount of time to help protect someone else's property.

In a world that sometimes seemed less than friendly, it kind of helped renew his faith in humanity.

He was restocking a cooler with bottled water when a sudden raucous cheer rang out from a good distance away. Seconds later, the walkie talkie clipped to Nancy's belt came to life, static coming through the speakers before Barry's voice boomed through. "We've got her contained!"

The small group under the tents seemed to exhale a sigh of relief all at the same time before smiling and giving each other hugs and high fives. Darrin smiled and rolled his shoulders, feeling the tension that had been holding his muscles captive all day start to ease up.

He finished filling the cooler with water, figuring everyone would need it once they returned, and was just putting the last bottle in when the first group of firefighters began to arrive.

Daniel walked over to him and Darrin offered him a bottle of water, which the other man took and drank from greedily. Daniel wiped his mouth with the back of his hand and grinned. "Feels good, man."

"How bad was it?"

He shrugged, the movement anything but casual. "It could have been worse. Unfortunately it looks like there was a definite loss of livestock, and there's a pretty good swath of charred brush and cactus, but no structures were damaged and everyone's alive and healthy. Tired and sore, but healthy."

"How often does stuff like this happen?"

Daniel cut him a look of disbelief. "Okay, I realize you're kind of my boss but I don't hesitate to give Chase and Owen shit so I'm not going to treat you any differently, but seriously? Do you know nothing about the ranch or life out here?"

Darrin shrugged. "To be perfectly honest, no. I've always viewed it more as an investment than anything else, and I tend to leave investments to the experts."

Daniel took a slow sip of water and was quiet for a couple of minutes before saying, "Fair enough. I'm not sure I completely understand that, but I can kind of see where you're coming from. But to answer your question, wildfires are a fact of life out here. When you have hot, dry summers and little to block the wind, the smallest spark can easily turn into something that eats up hundreds if not thousands of acres. This is the first one we've had so far this year, thanks to a wetter than normal winter and spring, which definitely helped keep it from being worse than it was."

"And do you and Miranda usually jump in and help out?"

"I usually do, yes. This is the first fire we've had since Miranda joined the staff."

A weird mixture of pride and fear filled him. Where it had come from God only knew, considering he didn't really have any right to feel either of those things where Miranda was concerned.

"Listen, I know you have a thing for her, and I know she has a thing for you, too," Daniel said, jolting Darrin out of his thoughts, "but if there's one thing I've learned about Miranda it's that she's her own woman. And she's more than capable of taking care of herself—and everyone else—should the need arise. So I'll warn you now—if you lecture her when she gets back, you'll have blown your chance. And for some strange reason you actually have one."

Darrin shook his head. "Why would I lecture her for helping fight a wildfire?"

"Because it's dangerous? It's men's work?"

Darrin snorted. "And if there's one thing I know about Miranda, it's that she wouldn't do anything that would potentially harm others, wildlife, or the land. My guess is that whatever she did to help fight this thing, she did so with confidence and knowledge while taking into consideration any physical limitations that may or may not be present due to her gender."

Daniel took another sip of his water, his expression serious, before his mouth lifted into a smile. "Well I'll be damned. You might actually understand her."

"Understand her? Hardly. Respect her, though? Absolutely."

CHAPTER EIGHTEEN

Do you typically move fast in relationships, or do you like to take your time?

EXHAUSTION PULLED AT MIRANDA'S LIMBS AS SHE WALKED BACK to her room, the smell of smoke following in her trail.

Thank God they'd been able to get the fire contained.

Once in her room, she crossed over to the bathroom, where she promptly stripped down and then climbed into the shower.

She took her time, letting the hot water wash away the dirt and grime before washing her hair twice in a desperate attempt to remove the smoke smell from it.

Only when the water grew cold did she turn off the water and grab a towel.

She walked out of the bathroom to find Darrin standing in her doorway, wearing nothing but a pair of shorts and holding a bottle of water in one hand and a banana in the other. She snorted. He raised an eyebrow.

"I figured you might be hungry and thirsty."

"Thanks. And I am, but I don't know if I have the energy to even peel that banana, much less eat it."

He stepped further into her room and kicked the door closed with his foot. "Try, okay?"

She sighed and sat on the end of the bed, pulling her towel

tighter around her body. The bed dipped when he sat down beside her, and then he handed her the bottle of water, which he'd opened for her.

Usually, she would argue against the help.

She didn't need help.

She was strong.

She'd been taking care of herself and Trevor and a million other things on her own for years. She didn't need a man to help her.

So it kind of grated that such a simple gesture would have tears pricking at her eyelids.

She blinked rapidly and took a cautious sip of water, knowing better than to guzzle it. Sure, she'd made sure to drink constantly throughout the day, but if the cramps in her shoulders and calves were any indication she was at least a little dehydrated. And the last thing she wanted was to puke her brains out in front of Darrin.

No, thank you.

Once she'd taken a few sips and her stomach remained settled, she took a larger drink before handing the bottle back to him and taking the banana. Potassium and carbs.

Yum.

He watched her as she ate the fruit, and she was surprised to find it didn't make her feel uncomfortable.

"Thanks for not making any blow job jokes."

Darrin's smile made her stomach flutter. "I figured you needed the sustenance more than I needed banana smashed in my face."

His words made her heart squeeze, so instead of responding she finished eating, still feeling tired but not quite so exhausted. Her stomach growled, making her grimace. "Apparently my stomach thinks that banana isn't enough."

He nodded. "You need food. Let me see what I can throw together real quick."

"Darrin…"

He pressed a finger against her lips. "Let me take care of

you."

She wanted to argue, to tell him she could take care of herself.

But dammit, even the strongest women needed help every now and then, right? And when that help came in the form of an incredibly sexy and surprisingly sweet man?

She couldn't say no.

It would be rude.

He smiled, as if he knew the thoughts that were running through her head, then took the banana peel from her and walked out of her room, closing the door softly behind him.

She sighed as she fell back onto the bed.

She was in so much trouble.

Darrin usually considered himself to be a nice guy, at least to the people in his inner circle. Sure, he had to be a shark in his business life, but that didn't mean he had to be a dick in his personal life. That being said, he wasn't usually the type to want to take care of someone else.

Probably because he'd had his fill of taking care of others before he'd even been old enough to legally drive a car.

Something about Miranda, though, made him want to take care of her. He was self-aware enough to realize it was probably her toughness and independence that did it for him; if she'd been a helpless damsel in distress or a single mom looking for her next baby daddy, he wouldn't have even given her the time of day. But the fact that she was so fucking together and capable and strong?

That was apparently a combination that pushed all of his buttons—including some he hadn't even known he had.

Shaking his head as if that would clear it, he threw the banana peel in the kitchen trash can before opening the refrigerator to see what he could scrounge up quickly for both of them.

As he pulled ingredients out of the fridge and set them on

the counter, he wished he had the current ability to make her something that would totally wow her. Maybe broiled salmon, roasted sweet potatoes, and some sort of salad. Simple, yet delicious.

And, yeah, something he'd been told before was impressive.

So sue him—he had an undeniable desire to impress her.

Since he didn't have any salmon or the time required to roast sweet potatoes, he figured he would make due with sandwiches.

Miranda shuffled into the kitchen as he was turning to slide their plates onto the island, wearing nothing more than an incredibly short pair of boxers and a tank top. She was very obviously bra-less.

Forcing his gaze up to her face, he smiled and said, "I hope you're okay with sandwiches. I know it's not much, but I figured time was of the essence."

"You would be correct. In fact, I'll be amazed if I manage to make it through this without passing out."

Hoping that conversation would help keep her awake long enough to finish her dinner, he asked, "So where'd you learn how to fight fires?"

She shrugged. "I volunteered with the wildfire department as an undergrad for a couple of summers, figured knowing how to help in case of a wildfire would be a good thing."

"That's not how college students usually spend their summers."

"I don't know that I was ever a normal college student. I knew what I wanted to be from the time I was in the third grade and a wildlife biologist came in and talked to us on career day. Somehow I never wavered in that. I started college with something like twenty-four credit hours already, and I pretty much kept my head down, went to class, and found volunteer or job opportunities that I thought could teach me something useful for my career."

"So you chose to fight wildfires over your summer break?"

"Along with taking summer classes, yeah," she grinned.

He shook his head. "That is some dedication. I didn't really have any idea what I wanted to be when I grew up until I was already in college."

"That sounds pretty normal to me. Like I said, I wasn't exactly the typical college student. Well, up until I got pregnant. Even I wasn't immune to making the occasional mistake."

"Trevor doesn't seem like a mistake, though."

She shook her head. "No, of course not. I mean, I made a mistake—unprotected sex can obviously have consequences—but I've never thought of Trevor in that way." She picked at what was left of her sandwich. "I was barely pregnant when I graduated, and even though it was hard as hell I wasn't going to let a bump in the road deter me from my goal. And I totally sound like I'm tooting my own horn now."

"Not at all. The way we respond to adversity says a lot about our character."

"So what about you? Any bumps along your road to greatness that I don't already know about?"

A snort escaped before he could stop it. He shrugged. "A few. But we all have crap we have to deal with on the way to achieving our dreams."

"I showed you mine, aren't you going to show me yours?"

Even with as tired as he was, her teasing tone and words had him at half-mast in less than a second. "I don't know that you have the energy for that right now."

Her cheeks turned red, but she laughed as she buried her face in her hands. "Ugh. I totally didn't mean it that way, but I obviously need some sleep."

"Go on and go to bed, I'll clean up in here."

She stood up and held out her hand. "Just leave it for in the morning and come to bed with me instead?"

Even though he had no intention of having sex with her tonight, she didn't have to ask him twice.

CHAPTER NINETEEN

Do you like to keep things casual, or are you more the serious type?

WHEN MIRANDA WOKE UP THE NEXT MORNING, THE SMELL OF smoke still clung to her hair and soreness permeated her muscles. She stretched, and immediately froze when she felt an arm tighten around her midsection.

What the hell had she done?

It was one thing to have sex with Darrin—even if she still wasn't sure if they'd crossed an ethical line or not—but it was another thing entirely to spend the night just sleeping with him. Sure, the sex the night before last had been mind-blowing (to say the least), but waking up clothed next to him somehow made her feel more naked than she'd been when he'd been inside of her.

This was clearly a problem.

Before she could remotely attempt to formulate an appropriate reaction this morning, the sound of a door slamming and Trevor's voice yelling, "Mom! Mom!" had her sitting up and shoving Darrin's shoulder. He stirred, stretched, fluttered those incredibly long eyelashes, and she got momentarily caught up in his beauty before the sound of her mother's voice jolted her back to reality.

This could not be happening.

"You have to get up!" she hissed at him.

"Hmmm?"

"Darrin! You have to wake up!" she said a little louder, hoping her voice didn't carry into the hallway.

His eyes finally opened, and he smiled up at her, all sleepy sexiness, and her stomach fluttered. She fought against the reaction and said, "Trevor's home and my mom's with him. You've got to get up."

She heard footsteps pounding down the hall, and knew that Trevor—in his usual fashion—would come bursting into her room at any moment. She shoved at Darrin so hard he almost tumbled off the bed.

"Quick! Go hide in the bathroom."

Looking sexy, sleepy, rumpled, and confused, Darrin shook his head and climbed out of bed before making his way to the bathroom. He closed the door behind him just as her bedroom door flew open.

"Mom! There was a fire!" Trevor exclaimed before launching himself onto the bed.

She wrapped her arms around him and breathed in his little boy scent. "I know, honey. I saw it."

"You did?"

"Sure did. How about I tell you all about it in a minute? I need to get dressed."

He slid off the bed. "Okay!"

The door closed behind him, and she shook her head at the whirlwind that was her son. She was pulling a t-shirt out of her dresser when the bathroom door opened and Darrin peeked through the opening. "Can I come out now?"

"Yeah. Sorry about that."

"It's okay. Believe it or not I do understand."

Dammit. Why did he have to be so decent sometimes?

"I just don't want to confuse him, or make him ask questions. And believe me, he would ask questions."

Darrin chuckled. "In the limited amount of time I've spent around Trevor, even I could have figured that out."

She smiled and closed the dresser drawer. "He's been like that ever since he learned to talk. It was like he went from saying 'mama' to asking me why the moon is in the sky all within a week."

She pulled her pajama top off and had her bra halfway hooked before she noticed the look on Darrin's face and realized what she'd done.

She was getting dressed in front of him. While having a conversation. Casually.

Like they'd been doing this for forever.

She ducked her head and finished fastening her bra before putting on the t-shirt she'd grabbed earlier. She debated changing out of her boxers into a pair of shorts for a split second, but then figured she'd already come this far, might as well go all the way. Through it all, Darrin stayed silent, a muscle along his jaw jumping ever so often the only thing letting her know he wasn't as unaffected as he seemed.

She pulled her hair back into a messy bun and said, "Let me get them distracted so they don't see you coming out of my room."

He nodded and swallowed, his Adam's apple bobbing up and down with the action. "No worries."

She nodded back at him, an awkward smile on her face that felt more like a grimace, and before she could say something incredibly stupid she walked out of her bedroom and closed the door behind her.

So much for avoiding complications.

Darrin let out a long, slow breath as soon as the bedroom door closed behind Miranda. He sat on the end of her bed and placed his head in his hands, wondering what the hell was going through her brain right now.

No, scratch that, he had a feeling he knew exactly what was going through her head right now—or at least the gist of it.

And he didn't like it. Not one bit.

Seeing Miranda the way he had this weekend had only served to open his eyes even more to the fact that she was one hell of a woman. Strong. Caring. Dedicated. Smart. Sexy as fuck. Stubborn. Independent.

To be fair, the list could go on and on.

The muffled sound of voices floated down the hallway and into the bedroom, and he pushed himself up off the bed before making his way over to the door. He cracked it open just enough to peek out and make sure no one was looking down the hallway before quickly closing the door behind him and making his way to his own room.

God, he felt like a teenager sneaking out of his girlfriend's dorm room at three in the morning again.

Shaking his head at the thought, he made his way to his suitcase where he grabbed a fresh change of clothes.

Fifteen minutes later he was showered and dressed. He'd just picked up his phone to shove into a pocket when it vibrated with an incoming text message.

Matt: How's the weekend going?

Darrin: Fine. How's yours?

Matt: How's Miranda?

How the hell did he know where he was? Darrin pinched the bridge of his nose before responding.

Darrin: I wouldn't know.

Matt: Dude, Sam told me everything.

If it wasn't for the fact that he knew just how easily women were swayed by Matt Roberts, he would threaten to cut his assistant's salary. Well, and if she wasn't the best damned assistant he'd ever had.

Darrin: Aren't you supposed to stop flirting with women now that you're married?

Matt: I didn't flirt. I simply asked.

Darrin: Yeah, right.

Matt: You still haven't answered my question, so I'm guessing your silence is consent in this case.

Darrin: She's fine.

Matt: Just fine? That's never a good thing when a woman says she's fine. FYI

Darrin: No shit. My words, not hers.

Matt: Oh. Well, in that case…

In that case, what? Darrin sighed and pocketed his phone. Matt was hands-down the best friend he'd ever had, but sometimes he drove him absolutely crazy. Like now. Now was definitely one of those times.

He ignored the vibrating phone in his pocket and walked towards the kitchen.

"I heard the fire was ginormous, Mom!" Trevor exclaimed as Darrin entered the room.

Three sets of eyes almost simultaneously turned towards him.

The first thing he noticed was Miranda's blush.

The second was Trevor's huge grin.

The third was that Miranda's mom looked weirdly familiar and brought to mind images of someone he'd long thought to be very firmly a ghost of his past.

CHAPTER TWENTY

Who are your biggest influences?

ONE SECOND MIRANDA WAS LOOKING AT DARRIN AND WILLING herself not to blush and feel like a giddy school girl, and the next she was picking her mom up off the floor where she'd landed after she'd fainted.

Darrin stood rooted to the spot as Miranda struggled to pick her mom up. She blew a hank of hair out of her eyes and looked up at him. "A little help here?"

He started as if coming out of a trance, but he walked over to them and scooped her mom up into his arms as if she weighed no more than a feather pillow.

To be fair, her mom wasn't exactly overweight, but she was definitely made from sturdy stock, so it was both unfair and sexy as hell that he was able to pick her up without so much as changing his breathing pattern.

Miranda pushed all thoughts of Darrin's sexiness out of her mind as he gently laid her mom down on the couch. Considering the expression on his face when he'd walked into the kitchen, Miranda fully expected him to run for the hills.

He gained a few more points by staying, even though something was obviously making him uncomfortable.

Trevor had followed them over to the couch, his bottom

lip caught between his teeth. "Is Granny gonna be okay?"

Miranda nodded as she checked her mom's pulse. It was steady, which was good. Honestly, she was more worried about whether or not she'd hit her head when she'd fainted than anything else. Her mom was in general good health, but she didn't exactly need a concussion, either.

Darrin pulled Trevor in close to his side, and Miranda couldn't fight the shock at seeing how easily her son relaxed into him. Why she was shocked, she wasn't sure; Trevor was generally a pretty trusting kid and had great relationships with Chase, Matt, and Owen, so why wouldn't he be comfortable with Darrin, too?

You haven't slept with Chase, Matt, or Owen, either.

Yeah, there was that.

Her mom stirring jolted her out of her thoughts, and Miranda sharpened her focus so that it was completely on her mother.

"What happened?" her mom asked as her eyelids fluttered open.

"You fainted, Mom."

She pressed a hand against her forehead. "I've never fainted before in my life!"

"I hate to break it to you, Mom, but you totally just did."

She tried to sit up, but Miranda gently held her down. "Take it slow. No need to rush, especially if you have a concussion."

"I didn't hit my head."

Miranda raised an eyebrow. "Are you sure about that?"

She nodded. "Yes. It feels fine, just a little fuzzy. No pain, though."

"Well, you're still looking pretty pale." Miranda looked at Darrin over her shoulder. "Could you go get her a glass of orange juice?"

He nodded and rushed back into the kitchen. Miranda turned her attention back to her mom, only to see that even more color had leached from her skin over the past few seconds.

"Mom? Don't pass out on me again."

She shook her head and then her body, like she was physically trying to shake something off. "I'm not."

A hand holding a glass of orange juice filled her peripheral vision, and then she heard Darrin say, "Here, Mrs. Jacobson, some orange juice might make you feel better."

Her mom's gaze cut to Darrin before swinging back to Miranda. "Thank you." She took a sip of the juice and closed her eyes. Took another sip. As her color slowly started coming back, Miranda felt her muscles begin to relax just a little bit.

Once her color was fully back, Miranda rocked back on her heels and looked from her mom to Darrin and back again. The tension in the room was so thick you could cut it with a rusted butter knife.

"I'm not sure I want to know what's going on, but does either of you feel like telling me?"

Darrin drew in a deep breath and sat on the edge of the coffee table, gravity and the weight of years of memories and old wounds pulling him down. He couldn't take his eyes off of Miranda's mom.

A woman who very obviously wasn't her biological mother considering Miranda was a blonde-haired white girl and Mrs. Jacobson was a dark-haired black woman.

A dark-haired black woman who looked exactly like the best friend of the woman who'd left his dad—and her children—so many years ago.

His gaze lifted up to Miranda, and belatedly realized that things were about to get really complicated and possibly really, really fucked up.

Before he could speak, though, Mrs. Jacobson spoke first. "You look a lot like your dad."

"After twenty years that's all you have to say?"

"You don't know, do you?" she asked softly, her eyes filling with sadness.

"Know what?" Miranda asked. "What the hell is going on?"

Darrin folded his hands together and looked at the woman across from him. "I'm kind of curious about that, too."

Mrs. Jacobson's hands wrapped around the edge of the couch cushions. "Something tells me this is going to be a very long story."

Miranda sat beside Darrin on the coffee table, her leg bumping against his. "So spill it, Mom."

Her gaze darted between Miranda and Darrin, and her mouth formed a very quick "O" before she managed to school her features. She cleared her throat and began to speak, looking at Darrin as she did so.

"First, let me clear something up—I never once condoned your mother's behavior and what she did to you, your sisters, and your dad, abandoning all of you like that."

Miranda drew in a sharp breath beside him. "Mom, how do you know Darrin's mom?"

"We were best friends since grade school."

"Were?" Darrin asked at the same time Miranda said, "Wait. Aunt Patsy was Darrin's mom? What the actual fuck?"

"Mama, you're not supposed to say the f word," Trevor said from where he sat on the other end of the couch.

All three of them swiveled their heads towards him and Miranda said, "No, honey, I'm not. Why don't you go to your room and play?"

Trevor stuck his bottom lip out, but didn't argue. Once he'd shut his bedroom door behind him, Miranda turned back to her mom and said, "Okay, I think we need to start from the beginning here, because there's clearly a lot of shit I don't know."

"You're not the only one," Darrin muttered.

Mrs. Jacobson sighed. "I don't know all the details, but yes, Darrin is Patsy's son."

Miranda shot up from the coffee table. "Oh my God I had

sex with my cousin?!"

"He's not technically your cousin, Miranda. Patsy and I weren't related by blood—or marriage for that matter."

Darrin held up a hand. "Can we just back up for a minute here? You said you and my mother were best friends. Does that mean she's…gone?"

Mrs. Jacobson nodded. "Yes, Darrin, it does. She passed four years ago."

He waited for the news to hit him, for him to feel something. Anything.

It never came.

"May I ask how? What happened?"

"Car accident. She was hit by a drunk driver."

"Now there's some irony," he muttered.

Miranda snorted.

Mrs. Jacobson looked between the two of them and said, "Yes, it was ironic, but there's no need for snarkiness."

"Sorry," Miranda said quietly.

Darrin didn't apologize. His mother had been a drunk and then a druggie, so her being taken out by a drunk driver was a very screwed up sense of poetic justice.

"At any rate, she's gone. When your dad didn't show up at the funeral I figured either he was still too angry with her for walking out or didn't know. I'm guessing he didn't know."

Darrin shrugged. "If he did, he obviously didn't say anything to me or my sisters."

"How are the girls doing?"

"Fine."

Mrs. Jacobson exhaled, her body almost deflating with the motion. "I realize you probably only vaguely remember me, Darrin. I was around a lot right after you were born, very much the proud godmother and surrogate aunt—your mom and I had always been more like sisters than friends, and a lot of people thought we were actually sisters because we looked so much alike. At any rate, we moved to Del Rio and away from Beaumont, and the visits became fewer and further between. My husband and I—Miranda's dad—started trying to conceive around the same time Patsy got pregnant with her second child. We were never able to get pregnant, and I admittedly pulled even further away because it was so hard to see my best friend and soul sister carrying and giving birth to healthy babies while every single month I once again found out I wasn't going to be a mother. We'd just adopted Miranda when your mother left your dad, and we didn't know she had for months, until one day she showed up on our doorstep with a suitcase and the clothes on her back.

"We took her in for a while, but once it became clear she was using we kicked her out. I'd had no idea she'd spiraled that badly. Where she went after that I have no idea, and it was years before she came back around. That was ten years ago, and she'd cleaned up her act, gotten sober and was getting her life back on track. She was actually on her way home from an AA meeting when she was hit and killed."

Darrin rubbed a hand over his face before looking at the woman across from him. He didn't know what to say. It was a lot to take in all at once.

Miranda sat back down beside him. "Mom, that still doesn't negate the fact that I slept with the son of the woman I've considered an aunt for most of my life."

He laughed. He couldn't help it. His entire world had just tilted on its axis and that's what Miranda chose to fixate on.

Not that it wasn't important, because it was.

"At least we're not actually cousins."

She smacked him on the arm. "Seriously?"

"You're a scientist. You should be able to figure that one out."

"Ugh. Of course I understand it from a biological perspective, and we obviously don't share any of the same common ancestry and genetics. But that doesn't negate the weird factor involved."

Instead of responding to Miranda, he asked her mom, "What's your name? I feel really weird calling you Mrs. Jacobson and not knowing your name, considering you were my mom's best friend and all."

"You don't even know your mom's best friend's name? Jesus. How fucked up was Aunt Patsy back in the day?"

"Miranda..." her mom warned.

"What? It's never been any secret that Aunt Patsy had issues."

Darrin snorted. "That's a nice way of saying it. There are obviously some gaps, but she was a druggie and an alcoholic, and like I've mentioned before, she just up and left one day."

"You said you were about eight, right?"

"Somewhere around there."

"So you were around eight years old when Aunt Patsy left, but you don't know my mom's name?"

He shrugged again.

"In Darrin's defense, the last time I saw him he was probably around five or six years old, and I'm guessing Richard didn't exactly talk about Patsy—or me—much after she left."

"Not really. I mean, Dad's never badmouthed my mother, and he's always answered questions as best he could, but he hasn't exactly had a reason to reminisce about the good ol' days."

"And to answer your question, my name's Betsy."

"Well, Betsy, it's nice to meet you. As an adult."

She smiled, and Darrin wondered what life would have been like had his mom not been a total fuck up, because at one point in her life she'd obviously been capable of making at least a few good decisions.

"And it's so good to see you...even under somewhat awkward circumstances."

"You think?" Miranda muttered before standing up. Her hands went to her hair, and then over her face and into her back pockets. "I've gotta...I'll be back. I just...need some air."

Before either Darrin or Betsy could say anything, Miranda was out the front door, the heavy wood closing quietly behind her. He turned to Betsy and gestured towards the door. "Should I…?"

Miranda's mom—hell, his mom's fucking best friend—shook her head. "Let her go for a little while. Sometimes she just needs space to think. Always has."

CHAPTER TWENTY-ONE

How important is family to you?

SHE'D SLEPT WITH HER HONORARY AUNT'S SON.

Of all the things she'd ever done to completely screw up her life, having sex with a messed up woman's son had never remotely been on the radar.

Clearly she and sex just shouldn't mix.

First, she got knocked up and abandoned, and then he had the nerve to freaking die in Afghanistan.

And then she slept with Darrin.

Who up until about fifteen minutes ago had been the best sex she'd ever had.

Not that she had much to compare it by, but she was pretty sure multiple orgasms counted as good sex.

She wasn't sure who she'd pissed off, but someone obviously had cast a spell on her or had a voodoo doll somewhere or something. Because this stuff didn't happen to normal people.

Sure, she knew that everyone had their crap they had to face, but this? She was pretty sure that unknowingly sleeping with your mom's godson topped almost everything.

Miranda opened the door to the office she shared with Daniel, and plopped down in the chair behind her desk. She stared at the stuffed bobcat on the shelf behind Daniel's desk and chewed on the inside of her cheek.

Her thoughts were tossing around in her head like yucca fronds during a thunderstorm.

Focus. She needed to focus.

With way more effort than it usually took, she pushed her emotions aside and looked at the facts before her.

Fact: Darrin was her mother's godson.

Fact: Darrin's mother was a woman she'd thought of as an aunt almost her entire life.

Fact: She and Darrin weren't actually cousins or related in any way, shape, or form.

Fact: Her mom knew Aunt Patsy had abandoned her children and had never said a word about it.

Scientist Miranda realized it was a complicated situation with many different layers.

Woman Miranda was a little freaked out by this particular twist of fate.

She was still staring at the bobcat when the office door opened and Daniel stepped inside. He stopped just in front of the door. "Are you okay?"

A hysterical laugh bubbled up her throat, making her clap a hand over her mouth. She shook her head. Nodded it. Shook it again.

Daniel sat down in his desk chair and propped a booted foot on his opposite knee. "I get it if you don't feel comfortable talking to me, but I've been told before that I'm a great listener."

She snorted then buried her head in her hands. "I'm just having a teeny tiny little crisis, that's all."

"Crisis? Crisis is my middle name."

She laughed. "I'm not sure even you would have experience with this type of crisis."

"Okay…"

She thunked her forehead on the desk and mumbled, "Darrin's my Aunt Patsy's son."

"Aren't you adopted?"

She raised her head and glared at Daniel. "You've seen my mom. I am very obviously adopted."

"Well, yeah, obviously. So how do you know Darrin's your aunt's son?"

She raked her fingers through her hair. "It's a long story."

"So tell me."

She debated giving him all the sordid details for about thirty seconds, and then Woman Miranda pushed Scientist Miranda out of the way and got to talking.

When she was done, she looked over at Daniel, only to see his shoulders shaking with silent laughter.

"You're seriously laughing at this?" She stood up. "Forget I even said anything."

He reached out and grabbed her hand. "Wait, Miranda, sit back down. I'm not laughing at you."

"Bullshit."

"I'm laughing at the situation. I mean, seriously. Take a step back from it all and look at it. This right here is proof that truth really is stranger than fiction sometimes."

She sat back down and mulled his words over. "It really is weird, isn't it? This is some sort of shit I would expect to see on a soap opera, not in real life."

"Well, the inspiration for those soap operas has to come from somewhere."

"True."

"So do you want my opinion or did you just need to vent?"

She sighed. "Both?"

"Fair enough." He sat back in his chair and drummed his fingers on his desk. "Here's the thing, I know it's pretty weird, but my guess is that what's really freaking you out is the fact that a woman you'd known almost your entire life had a life you never even knew about. Not to mention the fact that your mom is Darrin's godmother and this is the first you're hearing of any of it. That's enough to throw anyone."

"Yeah..." she conceded.

He leaned forward and dropped his voice, his tone gentle. "And my guess is that the other reason you're freaked out is because you really like Darrin, and this further complicates an already complicated situation. Plus, it's been a really eventful past couple of days. Less than twenty-four hours ago we were fighting a wildfire, for crying out loud."

And less than twenty-four hours prior to that she'd had the most amazing sex in her life. After kissing the man she was currently talking to.

"This might go down as the most eventful weekend in my life."

He grinned. "Years from now you'll look back on the past couple of days and laugh."

"Or cry."

"Or that, although it's hard to imagine you crying over too much."

She picked at her thumbnail. "I guess I'm not exactly girly, am I?"

"Miranda, look at me."

She lifted her gaze up to his.

"No, you're not girly, but you are all woman, and Darrin's lucky to have you even for a little while. And I swear to God, if he hurts you, I'll make him pay. I don't care if he's partially responsible for my salary."

Her cheeks warmed, but she couldn't quite hide the grin that teased the corners of her mouth. "Thanks, Daniel."

"You're welcome. Now get back to the house and figure out what you're going to do about your god-brother."

"I don't think that's actually a word."

He shrugged. "So I made one up. It'll probably be on Urban Dictionary within the week."

She laughed as she stood, feeling slightly better than she had just thirty minutes ago.

She was halfway out the door when she stopped and looked back into the office. "Hey Daniel?"

"Yeah?"

"The right woman is out there for you, and she's going to be one lucky chick. Just saying."

He nodded his head in acknowledgement, and she closed the door behind her.

CHAPTER TWENTY-TWO

What's your idea of romance?

"DARRIN, WHAT ARE YOU DOING?" MIRANDA MURMURED THE NEXT day as she closed the door behind her, a large bouquet of flowers cradled in her arms.

Never mind the fact that she hadn't even looked at the card yet—Darrin was the only person she could think of who would send her flowers and pay to have them delivered all the way out here.

She set the arrangement on the kitchen island and plucked the card out of its plastic holder, a riot of emotions warring inside of her heart and mind.

The feminine part of her wanted to bury her nose in the fragrant blooms and savor their scent. The cynical part of her figured he probably sent flowers to every woman he slept with.

She wasn't sure she liked either of those voices that were vying for attention.

Frustrated with herself, she opened the card.

I think I'm falling in love with you.

Her eyebrows drew together. Seriously? After one weekend of—admittedly hot—sex and crazy revelations he thought he was falling in love with her?

Hell, he probably used that line on everyone.

She tossed the card onto the island.

In love with her? He barely knew her!

He was in lust—not love. Nothing more. Nothing less.

Love would be crazy.

Darrin looked at his watch for the fifth—okay, fiftieth—time that day, wondering why he hadn't heard from Miranda yet. It was just after 5:30 and she'd signed for the flowers he'd sent at 1:32 this afternoon.

Surely she'd read the card by now.

With a sigh, he stood up and shoved his laptop into his briefcase. If he didn't find something else to do other than sit in his office he was going to drive himself crazy.

He'd just pulled the door shut behind him when his phone vibrated in his pocket. He looked, saw it was Matt, and answered the call as he made his way to the parking garage.

"Hey, what's up?"

"I'm gonna be a dad!"

Darrin chuckled. "I know that. I think the entire world knows that."

"No, I mean I'm going to be a dad today. Jenn's in labor."

"What hospital are you at?"

"Baylor."

"I'll be there in ten."

"Darrin, you don't have to. I know you have client meetings and dates and schmoozing and God knows what else you do in the evenings."

"Matt. You're my best friend. Yes, I do have to be there. I'll see you in ten." He ended the call and made his way to his car as fast as he could without running, glad his office was only a few miles from the hospital.

Once on the hospital's campus he made his way to Garage 4, parked, and then headed towards Jonsson, figuring he should be able to find Labor and Delivery from there.

After several wrong turns and elevator stops, he finally found Chase and Jo, who he hadn't seen since right after the transplant. The shadows under Jo's eyes had cleared and above his surgical mask Chase's skin was pinker and healthier looking than Darrin had ever seen it. He also looked like he'd gained back some of the weight he'd lost over the past few months, along with a couple of extra pounds.

It looked good on him.

He approached them, a smile on his face, but before he could even say anything Jo held out a plastic bottle and said, "Hand sanitizer."

He grinned and let her squirt the green gel into his hands. "Yes, ma'am."

"She's still a little overzealous with the soap and sanitizer," Chase joked, his voice slightly muffled behind the mask.

"That's okay and understandable. You look great, though, even with the whole Michael Jackson standing on a balcony thing going on."

Chase laughed. "Yeah, the surgical mask feels like overkill sometimes, but we're still getting my anti-rejection meds adjusted and I'm not willing to risk getting sick right now. The good news, though, is that I feel great. I haven't had this much energy in years."

"Poor guy. He has all this energy but he's still on lifting and activity restrictions."

"How long will that last?"

"Too damn," Chase said dryly.

Darrin chuckled. "Any word on Jenn? Has Matt lost his shit yet?"

"They actually just kicked us out of the delivery room because she's at a seven," Jo said.

"So she's close."

He'd been through this far too many times with his sisters and knew far more than he really wanted to about how much a woman's cervix dilated during childbirth.

"That she is."

"Are y'all's parents on the way up? What about Jenn's parents?" he asked Chase.

"Matt told the helicopter pilot we keep on standby for the ranch that he'd pay him ten times his usual rate to get them all here from the ranch ASAP. Unfortunately, from there to here is a little bit further than the helicopter can actually go on a tank of gas. When Mom and Dad found out he was trying to get a private jet at the Del Rio airport, Mom threw a fit and told him they would drive and be here as soon as they could."

"And Jenn's parents don't fly, so they're also driving up," Jo said.

"This should be interesting," Darrin said.

"Oh, the diaper battles have already been quite epic."

"Diaper battles?"

"Jenn's all about the wonders of modern manufacturing technology, whereas her mom is old school, cloth diapers all the way since cloth will always be available but disposable diapers might not be."

Jo continued, "But when Jenn pointed out that disposable diapers can be used for soil conditioner, flood control, and DIY ice packs she eventually got her mom to come around to the dark side."

Darrin laughed. "I cannot wait until they get here."

"Yeah, you can," Jo said, her tone dry.

"Oh, and Owen's already on his way up—Jenn called him this morning before her water even broke," Chase said.

"What about Caridad?"

"Isn't she filming that TV show?"

Darrin barely resisted slapping himself. "That's right. I totally forgot that started last week."

Chase looked at him quizzically. "Are you okay? It's not like you to forget something like that."

"I'm fine. I've just had a lot going on, is all."

Like the best sex of his life, helping people fight a wildfire, finding out his mom was dead, and realizing he was falling in love with a woman who apparently didn't share that same sentiment.

Just a typical, lazy weekend.

"I would imagine that being Dallas' Most Eligible Bachelor is keeping you pretty busy these days."

"Something like that."

Chase looked at him quizzically, but before the other man could say anything Owen rushed into the waiting room, his red hair standing on end and a frantic look on his face.

"She hasn't had the baby yet, has she? I didn't miss it, right?"

Jo grabbed his hands and squirted sanitizer into them. "No baby yet. She's at a seven last we heard."

"At a seven? What does that even mean?" Owen asked.

Jo squeezed his arm. "It means her cervix is dilated seven centimeters."

His eyes widened and he held up his hands. "Okay, that's all I need to know. I do not need to think about my best friend's cervix. She's like a sister to me, for crying out loud!"

Darrin chuckled and Chase outright laughed out loud, causing Owen to hang his head sheepishly. "It's okay, make fun of me all you want."

"I think it's sweet," Jo said.

"I think it's borderline crazy," Chase said before pulling Owen in for a hug. "It's good to see you."

Owen stepped back and smiled. "It's good to see you, too. You're getting fat, man."

Chase rolled his eyes. "It's called Prednisone. And, y'know, actually having a functioning kidney."

"Yeah, that whole functioning kidney thing might have something to do with it."

"Not to mention his appetite. I haven't seen him eat so much since we were kids," Jo said.

"It's the first time I've really had an appetite in months if not years. I honestly didn't realize just how bad I'd been feeling."

Jo wrapped an arm around her husband's waist and laid

her head on his shoulder. "I'm just glad you feel good now and do have an appetite."

"No kidding. You were starting to look a little like Skeletor," Owen joked.

Darrin's phone vibrated and he looked down to see the beginning of a text from Miranda. A little too eagerly, he unlocked his phone and opened the message.

Miranda: Thank you for the flowers. They're beautiful.

He waited to see if three little dots appeared below that message indicating she was still typing, but nada.

He told her he was falling in love with her and all she could say was thank you for the flowers?

That was it?

He pinched the bridge of his nose and closed his eyes, trying to get himself under control.

She'd turned him into some overly emotional version of himself, a man desperately needing a woman in order to feel happy and whole and complete.

He wasn't sure he liked it.

He also had a sinking feeling there wasn't much he could do about it, either.

Caridad: Not sure if anyone's told you, but Jenn's in labor.

Miranda looked down at the text message and smiled.

Miranda: Awesome! Any word on how she's doing?

Caridad: Owen just got to the hospital and said she's at a 7. Whatever that means.

Miranda snorted.

Miranda: LOL That means she's fairly close to having a baby.

Caridad: Obviously.

Leave it to Caridad to not know anything about the progressions of childbirth.

Miranda: Keep me posted?

Caridad: Sure.

Trevor ran into the house moments after she'd set her phone down. "Mama! Mama! Guess what Daniel found?"

"I have no idea. What did Daniel find?"

He grabbed her hand and tried to drag her towards the door. "Come see!"

She allowed him to drag her out of the house and to the barn that housed Daniel's loft, and immediately heard Daniel's laughter followed by a sharp bark.

Seconds later, she saw him—and a large ball of tan and white fluff—on the floor of the barn.

"It's a puppy, Mama! And Daniel said I could name it!"

She gave Daniel a stern look as she and Trevor joined him and the puppy. "You just found a dog?"

Daniel rubbed the fluff ball's ears. "I did. I was driving back from town and saw this little girl sitting on the side of the road next to what looked to be her mama."

"Was the mom…?"

He nodded. "Yeah. So I couldn't leave her there to get run over."

"Of course not." She sunk to the ground. The puppy saw her and immediately bounced over, all ears and tongue and fluff. And of course, she couldn't not love on it and laugh at the puppy's squirms of pleasure.

"She sure is clean for a dog you found on the side of the road."

Daniel shrugged. "I gave her a bath as soon as we got home."

"And I helped dry her off!" Trevor said.

Daniel ruffled his hair. "And you did a great job."

"Thanks."

The puppy lost interest in Miranda and ran to Trevor, causing him to squeal with delight as it crawled all over him.

"So, ah, I'm guessing this dog is yours?" she asked Daniel.

He shrugged. "I figured she could be the ranch's dog, if that's okay with you."

She wrapped her arms around her knees and smiled at Trevor and the puppy. "Yeah, that's okay with me. Trevor's been wanting a dog for months now, anyway. And it really is an adorable ball of fluff."

"I'm pretty sure that adorable ball of fluff is going to turn into a really big ball of fluff if her paws and those double dew claws are any indication."

"Maybe they should have named this place The Great Pyrenees Ranch rather than The Devils Ranch."

"The Gentle Giant Ranch."

"The Fluffy Ranch."

"Now that just sounds dirty."

"Better than The Furry Ranch."

They both laughed until they had tears coming out of their eyes, and only after their mirth had quieted did Miranda lower her voice and say to Daniel, "Darrin sent me flowers today."

"Well, he does seem like a pretty smooth sort of guy."

"Is that code for player?"

Daniel scratched his chin. "Kind of."

"He said he thinks he's falling in love with me."

"Okay, I hadn't seen that one coming."

"Neither did I."

He nudged her with his shoulder. "Oh, come on. We're dropping at your feet like flies here."

She snorted. "Because that's the image I want to associate with both of you."

"You know what I mean. And you're not giving yourself enough credit."

"It's not me, but more him. He barely knows me. How can he think he's falling in love with me?"

Daniel held up his hands. "I'm probably the last person you should be talking to about that."

"Fair enough." She blew out a breath and then raised her voice to a normal speaking level. "By the way, Jenn's in labor."

"Aunt Jenn's having the baby?" Trevor looked up from

the puppy long enough to ask.

"She is."

"Can I see her?"

Miranda shook her head. "She's all the way up in Dallas, sweetie. It would take us a while to get up there."

"How long?"

She sighed. "Really long."

His lower lip jutted out. "But I want to meet my girl-friend."

She rested her forehead on her knees and muttered, "Oh sweet baby Jesus. I am going to kill Jenn."

Daniel laughed, causing her to mutter some more and think that maybe she was the only sane person around these days.

CHAPTER TWENTY-THREE

What's your definition of happiness?

"IT'S A GIRL!"

Matt's exclamation had multiple heads turning towards the double doors that led back to labor and delivery, and the group gathered in the waiting room surged to their feet as one to offer the new father congratulations.

Sarah dabbed at her eyes with a tissue, her smile brilliant even after what had to have been a very long day.

Bo slapped his son's back, his eyes misty.

More hugs and back slaps and congratulations were exchanged, with everyone chattering excitedly.

"So when can we go back and see her?" Jo asked.

"Most importantly, does my granddaughter have a name yet?" Sarah joked.

Matt smiled. "Kaitlyn Antonia Roberts. And the doctor said to give them a few minutes before I brought everyone back."

More hugs were exchanged, and Darrin clapped Matt on the back. "Congrats, man."

"Thanks, D."

Before more could be said, Matt was swallowed up by the rest of the group, who peppered him with questions about what the baby looked like, how Jenn was doing, how he'd handled Jenn being in labor, if he'd watched the entire thing…

Darrin smiled and shook his head, taking in the scene before him.

Just a year ago, Matt had been a confirmed bachelor, living the life of a high-profile major league pitcher. And now, here he was, a husband and dad. The transformation from single guy to family man had happened quickly, and yet the difference wasn't jarring.

Family life looked good on his best friend.

Darrin pulled his phone back out of his pocket and checked it again, even though he knew he hadn't received any additional messages from Miranda.

He wasn't usually the type to second-guess himself. All his life, he'd set goals and done whatever it took to achieve those goals. He'd worked hard. Studied harder. Built a business from the ground-up and become one of the most well-respected and sought after sports agents in the country.

Doing that—finding success—had taken a certain sort of tunnel vision and dedication. One that hadn't left a whole lot of time for anything beyond casual relationships.

Sure, he'd forged some bonds with some people—Matt being one of them—but for the most part his life had started feeling a little bit…empty.

He'd never given much thought to relationships beyond that.

Until he'd been interviewed for the Dallas' Most Eligible Bachelor feature and the reporter had asked him far too many questions about his personal life, what he looked for in a woman, if he had plans for marriage and children or planned on staying a bachelor.

He'd given the reporter answers he figured she—and the readers—wanted and talked about how he looked for intelligence and a sense of humor, yes, he would love to get married and have a family some day if the time was right, no he wasn't currently dating anyone.

And even though at the time he'd told himself the answers were mostly bullshit, deep down he'd known they weren't.

The truth was, he was lonely.

Sure, he had friends and an interesting career, but in that moment he'd realized something was missing.

And then he'd met Miranda and Trevor and found those missing pieces.

She apparently didn't feel the same way, though, if her lack of acknowledgment of the card meant anything.

"Dude, you're staring at your phone like it just turned radioactive or said it doesn't like pizza or something."

"What?" Matt's voice jolted him out of his reverie, causing him to jerk his head up and almost drop said phone. "Sorry. Just have a lot on my mind is all."

"I know that look."

"What look?"

Matt stared him down like he was a rookie making his first plate appearance.

Darrin sighed and gave him his best deal-or-no-deal look.

Matt shook his head. "You know the look. The look of a man who's completely besotted with a frustrating woman who drives you crazy."

"Who are you? Lord Byron?"

"Hardly. I would much rather model myself after Mayer."

"Mayer?"

"As in John."

"I should have known."

"Or maybe Nathanson. Even Sheeran. They all have a way with words that just reaches in and grabs you."

"Have I told you lately how weird you are?"

"Eh, it's been a few weeks at least. So have you told her how you feel?"

Darrin rubbed a hand over his face. "Jesus, Matt."

"Take it from someone who almost lost the love of his life twice, D—sometimes being a man means opening yourself up. If you want happiness, if you love her the way I think you do, you've got to man up and just tell her."

"I did, okay?"

Matt drew his head back. "Oh. And?"

"Nothing. She said nothing."

"Wait. How did you tell her?"

Darrin looked down at the phone still in his hand.

"You sent her a text?"

"No! Even I'm not that romantically inept."

"Well, there's that at least. So…"

Knowing there was no way he was escaping this conversation, he looked around, made sure no one else was listening, and said, "I sent her some flowers this morning and wrote it on the card."

Matt looked at him so long and so strangely that Darrin began to seriously wonder if he's managed to grow an extra nose or something.

Finally, after long moments of what felt like judgmental silence, Matt closed his eyes and shook his head, making him feel like a six-year-old who'd just been pulled into the principal's office.

"You told her you loved her on a card?"

"Well, to be fair, what I actually said was, 'I think I'm falling in love with you.'"

"Because that makes it so much better." He sighed. "Listen, I've gotta get back to my wife and daughter and let visitors in before they stage a mutiny, but if you love her you've got to do better than that. Words are important, but women need to know you mean them. You have to show them."

"Alright, Dr. Phil."

"Dude, don't ever compare me to that crackpot again."

"He's a licensed psychologist."

"Who sold his soul to Oprah."

"Well who wouldn't? The woman's possibly more powerful than the leader of the free world."

"You have a fair point. Anyway. Come on back and meet Kaitlyn when you're ready, and then figure out how you're going to fix this little pickle you've found yourself in."

Darrin looked up at the ceiling and sighed. "You are so freaking weird," he said as he followed Matt back to meet the newest member of the Roberts family.

CHAPTER TWENTY-FOUR

Describe your perfect woman in a nutshell.

"So, YOU AND DARRIN MANN?" BETSY ASKED MIRANDA THAT FRI-
DAY evening as Trevor scampered off to the room his grandparents kept for him in their house.

Miranda set down his backpack and breathed deeply.
"Speaking of, how did I never know Aunt Patsy was married
and had children?"

"She didn't like to speak of it, at least not with most people."

"But she did with you."

Betsy nodded. "She did with me. It was kind of hard for
her not to, though, considering I'd been her maid of honor and
was the godmother of her first child."

Miranda looked down at the floor and shook her head.
"And how is it that you never reached out to them once you
knew Aunt Patsy had left them? I mean, I know it had to have
been difficult, but he was your godson, and I know how badly
you wanted children."

"I did. And I got you, which is the best thing that's ever
happened to me," Betsy said, hugging herself. "But I didn't
know that Patsy had just abandoned them. She told me they'd

separated and left it at that, and any time I tried to ask questions she would change the subject or apparently lie to me. When she told me she and Richard had separated and that he'd kicked her out of the house, I took her at her word. Ends up, I shouldn't have."

"Sounds to me like Aunt Patsy had some issues."

"To say the least. Mental illness wasn't something we talked about openly back when we were growing up, but I suspect that she was probably suffering from depression or worse."

"I'm pretty sure being an addict qualifies as worse."

"That's fair. It's not very nice, but it's fair."

"It's the truth, Mom."

"I know. I hated seeing her like that. Towards the end, those last few years of her life? That was the Patsy I'd known as a girl and been best friends with. It's still so hard sometimes to reconcile the two in my head."

"Drugs have a funny way of turning people into something they usually wouldn't be."

"Yes." Betsy blinked. "So, anyway. You and Darrin?"

"I really don't want to talk about this, Mom."

"Why not? He's a handsome man who seemed to be intelligent and honest, if not a little more polished than I would have expected you to be attracted to."

Miranda felt her cheeks warm and rolled her eyes. "I cannot believe you're wanting to have this conversation."

"I'm your mother, of course I do! And you haven't really dated or even shown much interest in anyone since Trevor was born. It's nice to see a little bit of sparkle back in your eye. So how did the two of you meet? Does he live in the area?"

And this was why she hadn't wanted to have this conversation. "Um, he's actually Matt and Caridad's agent, and good friends with them, too. And, uh, he's also one of the owners of the ranch."

"So what you're saying is he's your boss?"

Miranda barely resisted the urge to squirm. "Kind of. Yeah, he's one of the owners, but I'd never even met him until Matt and Jenn's wedding."

"So where does he live?"

"Dallas."

Betsy raised an elegant eyebrow. "And yet he was here last weekend?"

She shrugged. "He just randomly showed up. And before you start getting any additional ideas about me and Darrin, it was a one-time thing. We barely know each other."

Betsy gave her the "I'm your mother and know you better than that" look, making Miranda feel slightly uncomfortable. One, because she'd never been able to hide anything from her mom. Two, because she was pretty sure she'd given Trevor that same look on more than one occasion.

"Then get to know each other."

"It's not that easy, Mom. Did you miss the part about him living in Dallas and being a very high-powered sports agent? My life—and Trevor's life—is here."

"But Miranda…"

"There are no 'buts' with this, Mom. It was a temporary moment of insanity. That's it." She gentled her tone. "Now, I've gotta go. I'm meeting Owen and Caridad for a little while."

She and her mother exchanged hugs and kisses, and even though Betsy smiled and acted like she was okay, it was obvious she wasn't.

Miranda mulled over the conversation all the way from her parents' house to April's, a Del Rio bar everyone liked to hang out at occasionally.

It was a long five minutes.

Once she stepped into the dimly lit bar, though, she forced all thoughts of Darrin to the back of her mind. Tonight was for hanging out with friends and letting loose a little bit—not for obsessing over a man.

Caridad: The eagle has landed.
Darrin: What?
Caridad: You heard me. The eagle has landed.
Darrin: The eagle?
Darin: Oh. Got it.
Caridad: *rolling my eyes*

Darrin grabbed his keys and made his way out of Caridad's house and to his car.

He briefly felt bad about enlisting Caridad to help him ambush Miranda, but desperate times called for desperate measures. She'd barely responded to his texts and hadn't answered the couple of times he'd called her.

So with Matt's advice to show her how he felt playing on repeat in his head, he'd conspired with Caridad.

About ten minutes later he pulled into the parking lot of April's, the bar Miranda was meeting Owen and Caridad at. When he stepped inside it took him all of five seconds to find her.

She was dressed casually in jeans and a tank top, making him glad he'd opted for jeans and a t-shirt himself. Her back was to him, so he took a few brief moments to enjoy the view and take a deep breath before putting on his game face.

Miranda felt the hair on the back of her neck prickle with awareness, and shifted uncomfortably. As inconspicuously as she could she glanced around the bar, trying to figure out why she felt like someone was watching her.

Darrin walking towards their group was the last thing she'd expected to see.

Nervous—and kind of pissed off—she turned back to Owen and Caridad and quietly said, "Seriously, guys?"

Owen held his hands up, palms out. "Hey, I had nothing to do with this one. It was all Darrin and Caridad."

"Thanks for throwing me under the bus, Lumberjack. We'll see if you get any for a few days."

"Seriously? That's all you have to say?" Miranda asked.

Caridad shrugged. "He asked if I could help him, and I've never seen Darrin like this over a woman, so I said yes. Besides, a blind man could see you're equally gaga over him. Now shh. Get ahold of yourself."

Miranda rolled her eyes before taking a swig of her beer. She was sorely tempted to just walk out since she wasn't a fan of being manipulated, but a part of her kind of wanted to see how Darrin was going to explain this to her.

Plus, she'd just got her beer.

Darrin pulled up beside her, but instead of addressing the entire table he leaned over and whispered in her ear, "I'm sorry I ambushed you like this. Don't be mad at Cari—this is all on me."

She fought the shiver that worked its way down her spine and nodded her head.

Owen took one look at them and dragged Caridad out onto the dance floor, leaving them alone at the table.

"What exactly did you expect to accomplish here?" she asked with preamble.

"Talking to you. Apologizing to you."

"For what?"

"For the way I handled those flowers Monday."

"It was a beautiful arrangement. There's no need to apologize."

"You know what I'm talking about, Miranda."

"I do?" she asked innocently.

"Yes, you do. I shouldn't have told you what I did like that."

"What exactly did you tell me? Did I miss something?" She was so going to hell for this, but he needed to actually say the words. Even if she didn't believe them.

Well, quite believe them.

Couldn't believe them.

"They didn't include a card?"

She shrugged. "What did it say? It's been a long week."

He narrowed his eyes then shook his head and smiled.

No wonder his clients were some of the highest paid athletes in history—he could go from laser-focused to charmer in the blink of an eye. Opponents didn't stand a chance.

She, however, was made of stronger stuff.

No way was she buckling under pressure.

"The card should have said, 'I'm in love with you.'"

"I think you left out a few words." Dammit. Her response had slipped out before she'd had a chance to pull it back.

Darrin just smiled. "Well, the card did have a few more words, but I should've just said what I really wanted to say—that I'm in love with you."

"How can you be in love with me, Darrin? You barely know me."

"Is that what you really think?"

"Yes. We barely know each other."

"You say we barely know each other, but that isn't true at all, Miranda. I know that you're an intelligent, incredibly strong woman. You're fiercely independent and a great mom. You have an amazing sense of humor when you let your guard down. You're determined and ambitious, even though that ambition isn't obvious in the typical ladder-climbing ways. You love your job. Hell, you're more passionate about wildlife conservation than most people are about, well, anything. You're trustworthy and honest. You make amazing chicken and dumplings and snore a little when you sleep. You have a soft spot for mindless television but spend most of what little spare time you have contemplating the connection between moon phases and deer movement. You're incredibly giving, but you're scared to death to let yourself receive because you don't want to get your heart broken again. And you would literally face down a mountain lion in order to save your son. Do I need to keep going? Because I can."

Miranda took a long swallow of her beer, not sure how

to respond. It had been so long since anyone had remotely tried to get to know her on that level that she didn't…she just couldn't.

"Darrin…"

"Just think about what I said, okay? I do love you. And that's not exactly something I've said to a lot of people."

"I just…okay…say I accept what you're saying…that you love me. What do you expect to happen here? Your life and business are in Dallas. My life is here. Trevor's grandparents are here."

"It's just distance, Miranda."

"Because four hundred miles is just a short hop and a jump."

"There are these great things called helicopters and air-planes."

"The Del Rio airport doesn't really have commercial flights," she pointed out.

"But there are private and charter flights."

"Do you have any idea how expensive those are?"

He shrugged. "I'm sure I could negotiate some sort of rate."

"You have an answer for everything, don't you?"

"Pretty much."

"Darrin, I don't know."

"I know you don't. But how about we give it a try? I can keep my home base in Dallas and fly down here as much as possible. And I can fly you and Trevor up to Dallas some-times, too."

"I don't…this is crazy…you're crazy."

He grinned. "I know. Crazy about you."

"That was really corny."

"But you liked it."

"A little."

"Give me a chance?"

She stared down at her beer as she considered his words and her own feelings. The truth of the matter was, as much as she wanted to believe they didn't know each other, they did. Sure, there were little details they didn't know—like each other's favorite food or movie—but the important stuff was easy.

"I read your interview, the one about you being named Dallas' Most Eligible Bachelor."

"Oh?"

She nodded. "The interviewer left some stuff out."

"Like what?"

"Like," she licked her lips, "the fact that even though you had the odds stacked against you at an early age you didn't let that define you. You're successful, not only because you're smart and a great negotiator, but also because you're honest. You don't let people get too close to you—most likely because of an unconscious fear of abandonment—but the people you do let in are in for life. My son adores you and asks about you. And you would do anything for the people you care about."

"Well, it was a fluff piece."

She laughed. "Obviously. And she got it all wrong."

"She just wrote down what I told her. And one part was definitely right."

"What's that?"

"The part about what kind of woman I was looking for. I was describing you before I even knew you."

She felt her cheeks warm, but instead of saying anything, she responded by leaning in and capturing his mouth with hers.

When they pulled apart, she looked up at him and said, "I don't know that I'm in the love stage just yet—trust issues and all that jazz—but I do really, really like you and think that maybe I could get there with a little bit of time and persuasion."

He raised an eyebrow. "What kind of persuasion did you have in mind?"

"Well, Trevor's at my parents' house all weekend…"

"That sounds like a good start." He stood and grabbed her

hand, and as he pulled her away from the table yelled out to Caridad and Owen, "See you guys later!"

They left to hoots and catcalls—mostly from Caridad—laughing all the way to her truck.

"Now, about that persuasion?" he asked.

She pressed a button on the key fob and unlocked the truck. "Hop on in."

"Gladly."

She smiled all the way back to the Devils Ranch.

EPILOGUE

10 years later

Trevor looked out at the sea of caps and gowns, and then up to the stands where he knew his family was watching and waiting. With a smile, he leaned towards the podium and spoke into the microphone.

"Good afternoon, Class of 2026, family, and friends. I know that these things are usually long, boring speeches about how bright our futures are with maybe a Dr. Seuss quote thrown in for good measure, but this isn't going to be one of those valedictorian addresses.

"Instead, this is going to be a speech about family.

"A lot of you—okay, all of you—are probably wondering what family has to do with graduating from high school. After all, a lot of us come from what's commonly called a 'broken home.' Some of us have divorced parents. Some of us are in foster care. Some have even been adopted. Some have been raised by a single parent. But just because our homes might be broken, that doesn't mean that we have to be broken. Just because our family may not look like the family in the cereal commercial, that doesn't mean our family is less in any way.

"When I was eight years old, my mom met my Dad. I never knew my father, who was killed in Afghanistan when I was a baby. Even with that, though, I was lucky. Mom and I had a makeshift family of us and grandparents and friends that were my surrogate aunts and uncles and cousins.

"From them I learned that love and acceptance have nothing to do with blood and everything to do with the mind and the heart. I learned that love—and true family ties—can be really amazing and very, very hard to break.

"From my Uncle Matt, I learned how to throw a fastball—although not very well, I have to admit—and that loving someone sometimes means doing crazy things like donating a kidney or retiring just minutes after winning the World Series.

"From my Aunt Jenn I learned to appreciate books and words and stories even more than I already had, and our debates about the pros and cons of romance novels have been epic. By the way, I still think Larry Correia's books are better than any romance novel you've persuaded me to read, Aunt Jenn.

"From Uncle Chase I learned far more than I ever wanted to know about kidneys, but he's also taught me—by example—how important it is to never give up and that humor really is the best medicine.

"Aunt Jo has taught me what unconditional love looks like, and that we shouldn't settle for anything less.

"Aunt Cari taught me how to shoot, and that staying calm, cool, and collected isn't a bad thing.

"Uncle Owen's taught me how to build stuff—sorry about that time I smashed your thumb with a hammer—and that patience is definitely a virtue.

"And last, but certainly not least, Mom and Dad. I wouldn't be standing up here today if it wasn't for them. Sure, Mom always stayed on top of me to do my homework, but she also encouraged and nurtured my imagination. And not only did she give me life, she also literally saved my life. FYI, y'all, mountain lions are kind of scary up close and personal.

"And Dad…you treated me as your own from the beginning, and helped give Mom and me a life we never would have had otherwise. Because of you, Mom was able to pursue her doctorate degree, and I got to grow up around some really cool people. But most importantly, because of you, our family was whole. You were the missing piece.

"So to the class of 2026, as we leave the safety nets of high school and our homes, know that family is what you make it. No matter where you are. No matter your age, gender, or the color of your skin, family is what you make it. And as we look towards the future, I hope that we all remember that family and life don't often look like a Hallmark card—and that that's perfectly okay.

"Thank you, and congratulations to the class of 2026!"

Applause rang out as he stepped away from the podium, and as he sat back down he looked up to where his family was sitting—the family of his blood and his heart—and smiled.

***

Keep reading for an excerpt from the book that started it all:
Between the Seams

Enjoy what you read? Please consider leaving a review so other readers can discover great books, too!

Acknowledgments

This book admittedly took much longer for me to write than I'd intended, so I would be completely remiss if I didn't acknowledge that fact—and the readers who have stuck with me and still wanted Darrin's story.

Thank y'all.

Aubrey

P.S. Love what you read? Share the love and leave a review and/or rating so other readers can find books to read!

Want to Read more from Aubrey?
Check out the other books in the Devils Ranch
Series: Between the Seams, Baseball and Lessons,
and Hair Trigger Heart. And be sure to keep an eye
out for the first book in a brand new series, coming
soon!

Keep reading for an excerpt from the book that
started it all, and that readers are calling "a home
run" and "a grand slam!"

Excerpt: Between the Seams

What happens when life throws you a curveball?

Chase Roberts is the quintessential Good Guy. Attractive, athletic, intelligent and successful, the former college baseball star and one-time major league prospect is the kind of guy any woman would love to take home to Mama. Except there's one small problem: Chase has never really gotten over his former best friend—and first love—Jolene "Jo" Westwood, who broke his heart as a teen. Now, all grown up with two thriving businesses, Chase has enough to worry about.

Jo Westwood just wants to come home to Del Rio, Texas, help nurse her grandmother back to health and go back to her calm--okay, boring and lonely--life in Austin once the summer's over. Unfortunately (fortunately?), her best-laid plans come to a screaming halt the moment she accidentally bumps into her former best friend--and first love--Chase Roberts in the feminine hygiene aisle. The cute boy she once knew has become a HOT man. A hot man who seemingly hates her. Great.

As the long, hot summer drags on, Chase and Jo find themselves spending more and more time together, resurrecting not-so dead feelings and putting the past behind them. Unfortunately, summer only lasts so long, and even love may not be able to survive long-held secrets that threaten to tear them apart.

CHAPTER ONE

"Yo, Chase, did you hear a word of what I just said?"

Chase Roberts snapped out of his reverie and glanced over at Owen Daniels, his best friend, business partner and occasional pain in the ass. "Sure."

Owen snorted. "No, you didn't."

A pretty blonde entered the building across the street, and Chase fought the overwhelming urge to follow her. "Did you see the blonde across the street just now?" He asked instead.

Owen opened the driver's side door of his car. "I thought you'd sworn off women? Called them all second-hand groupies or something like that."

Chase looked at the building—Mitchell's Drug Store—one more time before climbing into the passenger seat of the low-slung Mustang. "I didn't say they were all second-hand groupies. There just happen to be more than I would like."

"Must be tough, being chased by hot, scantily-clad women all the time."

Owen pulled away from the curb and Chase fought the urge to turn and watch to see if the blonde came out of the drug store.

"It is when the only reason they're chasing after me is because of my brother." Chase's brother, Matt, was Mr. Baseball. The long-time ace for the Texas Wranglers, Matt was well-loved in their hometown of Del Rio, Texas. So well-loved the high school baseball fields now bore his name. Without a sponsorship. So well-loved that he had his own menu item at Francine's Diner. So well-loved that there was a freaking Matt Roberts Day, complete with a downtown parade. In November. After the World Series and before Winter Ball started. Hell, his brother had been given keys to the damned city.

As much as Chase loved his brother, he got tired of the groupies who decided that if they couldn't have Matt they would just settle for Chase. After one too many stories posted about him on internet message boards and questionable websites, Chase had decided about a year ago that maybe a female hiatus was in order.

Besides, he had a business to run, and even with his last name he still wanted to project the image of responsible, trustworthy businessman—not wannabe playboy.

"Boo-freaking-hoo."

Chase ignored Owen's sarcasm. "Anyway. Did you happen to see her?"

"Who? The curvy blonde going into Mitchell's?"

"Yes. That one. Apparently you did."

Owen shrugged. "She looked like she had a nice ass."

"She looked familiar."

Owen turned into the parking lot of Roberts Ventures, LLC, and swung into the space next to Chase's pickup. "Previous one-night stand?"

Chase snorted. "No. Definitely not one of those." Hell, Chase could count on one hand the number of one-night stands he'd had over his entire lifetime. His brother's groupies just made it sound like he was, well, a player.

They got out of Owen's Mustang and entered the building. Chase's executive assistant and all-around office goddess looked up and smiled at Chase. As soon as Kimberly's gaze landed on Owen, her smile quickly turned to a frown.

Chase didn't know why Kim didn't like Owen, and no amount of gentle prying had managed to get the information out of her. "Good morning, Kim."

"Mornin', Chase. We got the Sutton contract in, and Frank Wimbly called earlier, said he found a spot out by the lake that he would like to take a look at."

Chase nodded. "Thanks. I'll take a look at the Sutton contract and give Frank a call back."

He made his way to his office, shaking his head as the sound of Kim scolding Owen could be heard from down the hall.

Never a dull moment he thought as he got back to work.

☙

Jolene Westwood was usually pretty hard to embarrass. As a high school guidance counselor, she'd heard—and discussed—some of the most embarrassing things human beings experienced. From high school crushes to missed periods to kids grappling with their sexuality, she thought she'd heard—and seen—it all.

But embarrassment was much easier to deal with when it wasn't your own, and unfortunately she was currently knee-deep in it on this lovely evening.

She'd just been standing there, in front of the pads, tampons and Monistat cream that lined the back wall of the Del Rio Walmart, debating small pack versus value pack, when she accidentally backed up into someone.

A solid someone who radiated warmth and *man.*

Slowly, she turned around, her hands still paused mid-air, holding the bright yellow and blue boxes up like some sort of offering.

Or maybe as a big fat red light.

No pun intended.

Her gaze wandered up from the box of Crest toothpaste in one hand to the center of what was definitely a polo-clad male chest and up to a jaw shadowed with dark stubble. Firm lips. Slightly crooked nose. Brown eyes that made her think of warm, cinnamony Mexican chocolate. Dark eyebrows. Dark brown, almost black hair that curled out from under a blue YETI coolers ball cap.

Jo swallowed a gasp—or, more realistically, a long-ing-filled sigh—and took a quick step back.

Chase Roberts.

Childhood best friend.

Teenage crush.

The boy she'd long ago said goodbye to.

Her stomach flip-flopped as she slowly lowered her hands and her gaze. Mentally drank him in.

Six-one.

Two hundred pounds.

1.87 ERA.

At least, those had been his college stats. If anything, he looked like he might have gained a couple of inches, and whatever he weighed, it sure looked like it was pure muscle.

Realizing she was staring like an idiot, she mentally shook herself and somehow found her voice. "I am so sorry, Chase. I didn't see you behind me."

Stupid, Jolene. Of course you couldn't see him behind you, it isn't like you have eyes in the back of your head.

His melted chocolate gaze traveled up and down her body before settling on her face. "I'm sorry, you seem to have me at a disadvantage—you know my name, but I don't know yours."

Jo smiled, even though she was cringing on the inside, and she fought back the sense of disappointment his words evoked. They'd been friends for years and he didn't remember her? Hell, her mother had tried to end his parents' marriage, until the truth finally came out years later that Chandra Sommers had never slept with Bo Roberts. Ends up Sarah Roberts had known that for far longer than Jo had—Chandra was more than happy to let her daughter believe the worst. And he didn't remember her?

Serves you right, for ending things the way you did.

Her voice tinged with the disappointment she apparently couldn't hide, Jo responded. "Sorry. I've changed some since the last time we saw each other. Jolene Westwood."

Chase's brows drew together over those hot chocolate

eyes. "I feel awful, but I don't remember a Jolene Westwo—wait a second. Jo? Jo Sommers?"

Jo could feel her cheeks warming and knew she was probably beet red by now. Could this be any more awkward? "Sorry. I changed my name a few years back, after my parents died."

"Westwood is your grandma's name, right?"

Jolene nodded and swallowed. "Yeah."

Lame, Jolene, lame.

Chase stood before her, a brown-eyed god with a 92 mile per hour fastball and a nasty curveball, looking for all the world like a pitcher who couldn't understand a single one of the signals the catcher was sending him.

꙳

Jo. Jo Sommers. His childhood friend and teenage crush. The captain of the cheerleading squad and smartest girl in the room (and hell, their class).

He'd known it was her as soon as she'd turned around and allowed that sea glass gaze to travel up his body oh so slowly. He'd never be able to forget those eyes——they'd haunted him for so long they were a permanent part of his psyche at this point.

She may have changed a little bit—her blonde hair was softer, longer and wavier than he remembered, and she'd gained some curves since he'd last seen her when they were in college, but he sure as hell would never be able to forget her.

So why was he playing stupid now?

She'd fueled more than one of his teenage fantasies, even after she'd suddenly stopped talking to him their freshman year of high school. As a teen he wondered if it had to do with the health issues—and eventual scarring—he'd had as a kid and young teen. Had she been embarrassed to be around him?

As an adult, he realized there could have been other reasons, but even a cocky teenage athlete can be felled by one simple brush off from the prettiest girl in school.

"So, uh, what brings you back to town?"

Smooth, Roberts, real smooth.

Worry briefly turned those sea glass eyes stormy, but the expression was gone so fast he wondered if he'd imagined it.

"Gran had a hip replaced. She refused to go to a rehab facility, and pretty much ordered me to come take care of her." A small grin played at the corners of Jo's generous mouth, and for a brief second Chase was reminded of the girl she used to be. The one who'd been his playmate and confidante.

"How's she doing?"

Jo waved her hand, and then blushed as she looked at the box she still held.

"I'm really not trying to accost you with tampons, I swear."

Chase barely managed to choke back the laughter that threatened to escape. "Well, at least they're not used."

Jesus, Roberts, that was awful.

Her blush deepened, and the chuckle that had been threatening to escape somehow managed to rumble out. Jo shook her head, smiled, and tossed the box into her cart. "I'm glad to see you still have a sophomoric sense of humor, Chase."

"At times, yes." Unfortunately.

Their gazes met, held, and then a slow smile bloomed over Jo's face before she, too, was laughing. "How about we try this again?" She held out her hand. "Hey, Chase! Nice to see you again."

Chase wrapped his hand around hers, and he swore he felt tingles shoot up his arm. "Jo, it's good to see you, too."

Unsettled, he dropped her hand and stepped back. A look of confusion flitted across her pretty face before she once again replaced it with an odd, too-placid-to-be-real smile.

Had she felt it, too?

"Well, uh, I better get going." She gestured to her cart, which held a small amount of groceries and toiletries. "Gran's waiting for me to get back so I can cook supper. Can't let her starve."

Chase took another step back, feeling the need to put

some amount of distance between them. He flexed his hand, still feeling slight tingles in his fingertips. "No, can't let her starve."

Jo began to push her cart away, and before he could take the words back he blurted out, "We should do lunch some time. Or supper. Catch up. For old time's sake."

God, he sounded like an effing idiot. Catch up for old time's sake? Yeah, because *that* sounded like a brilliant idea.

An expression Chase couldn't identify clouded Jo's eyes before it, too, was gone almost as quickly as it came. "Um, sure." She nodded her head once, her wavy blonde hair falling over one shoulder. "We'll have to do that."

Chase nodded in ascent and shoved his hands into his pockets. Jo shot him one last glance before turning from him. Chase allowed himself to enjoy the view as she walked away.

Couldn't not appreciate it, really, as it was a damned fine view. The same damned fine view he'd seen just this morning walking into Mitchell's Drug Store.

᠃

"Jolene, is that you?"

Jo set down her grocery bags and blew a strand of hair out of her eyes. "Yes, Gran, it's me."

"Good, that rehab woman just left and I'm starving."

Jo rolled her eyes. "I think that rehab woman has a name."

"Yes, the Devil's Harlot!" Gran shouted back from the living room.

Jo sighed and yelled back. "She's not a harlot, Gran." Who even used the word "harlot" anymore? "She works for Val Verde Regional Medical Center. Last I checked, Satan wasn't on their payroll."

Gran harrumphed from the living room. Jo finished putting up the groceries and walked into the living room. "Did she make you do something new today?"

Her grandmother sat in a big, somewhat comfortable chair. She waved a hand in the air dismissively. "Just a new exercise. Nothing too bad."

"Then why the name-calling, Gran?"

Gran gestured towards the flat screen TV mounted on the wall across from her. "She was lusting after that Roberts boy. Acting like a cat in heat."

"Roberts boy? Chase? Why was Chase on TV?" Jo's mind went back to the embarrassing scene in Walmart, and realized it was a good thing Gran couldn't read her thoughts. Chase Roberts all grown up was definitely worth lusting after.

Gran waved the remote. "No, not the sick one, bless his heart. The older one."

Sick? Was Gran referring to Chase's childhood illness, or did he only look like the picture of health? Hot, hot health.

"And we're back at the top of the eighth inning, and Wranglers ace Matt Roberts is back out on the mound."

Jo looked at the television and saw Chase's older brother, Matt, readying the mound for another inning. The camera zoomed in on his face, and Jo had to admit that he was definitely attractive. Always had been. Problem was, he'd always known it, too.

While Chase had been popular and well-liked in his own right, Matt had always had that "it" factor that just drew people to him. Throw in obnoxiously good looks and talent that had scouts looking at him as a freshman, and you had a combination that was hard for any girl to resist.

"The PT was openly lusting after Matt in front of you?"

Gran pursed her lips. "The shameless hussy wouldn't shut up about him. Went on and on about how 'hot' he is. Cat in heat, I tell you!"

Jo loved her Gran, she truly did, and while Jo was by no means remotely promiscuous, her grandmother's old-fashioned views sometimes came across as a little, well, old-fashioned.

"Well, Gran, in all fairness he's not an unattractive man."

"Don't you start acting like a hussy too, Jolene!"

Jo sighed. "Gran, just because a woman thinks a man is attractive, that doesn't make her a hussy. Come on, you thought Pawpaw was handsome before you married him, didn't you?"

Gran's eyes misted over and a small smile tugged at her lips. "Oh, your Pawpaw was so handsome in his dress blues. He had the most beautiful eyes—that's where you get yours, you know—and the sweetest smile. Curly black hair. Such a fine figure the first time I saw him. I knew right then I was going to marry him."

Jo smiled. "You just proved my point, Gran."

The older woman shrugged and absently massaged her hip. "Always been too smart for you own damned good."

Jo leaned over and kissed her grandmother's wrinkled cheek. "And you know you wouldn't have it any other way, young woman."

Gran couldn't hide her smile. "Don't go getting a big head, young lady. Now what's for supper?"

ᕽᔭᑐ

Later that night, feeling restless and crampy and border-line maudlin, Jo climbed out of the full size bed in the room that had been her's as a teen and pulled a box from the top shelf of the closet. She set it on the floor, brushed the dust off and opened it.

Inside were high school mementos.

Her Homecoming mum from her senior year, the bells still shiny but missing a glittery letter from her name. A set of royal blue and white pom poms. The corsage Billy Walther gave her for senior prom, the roses dried and in a protective plastic case, the lilac elastic band's color still as vivid as the day he'd slid it on to her wrist. There were other pieces of flotsam and jetsam, memories of years gone by.

A newspaper article talking about how she'd made vale-dictorian. The notecards from her graduation speech. An old report card. Her acceptance letter to Baylor. Notes she and her best friend Jenn McDonnel had passed during algebra.

At the bottom of the box lay her senior memory book and

four yearbooks. She withdrew all of them and returned to the bed, leaving the other items on the floor where she'd left them.

She wasn't sure what had her feeling nostalgic. Maybe it was being back here in Del Rio, sleeping in the same room she'd slept in as a teen far too often when things went downhill at home. Maybe it was seeing Chase tonight. Or maybe Aunt Flo was just a mean bitch who made her do crazy things.

She opened the memory book, smiling at the memories and the thoughts of an eighteen-year-old girl hell-bent on changing the world. Or at least her little corner of it.

10 Years From Now I...
Will be Oprah's go-to psychologist on all of her shows
Will own my own practice
Will be married with two kids—boy and girl—to a gorgeous man who owns his own business, makes a lot of money and will never cheat on me
Will be a great mom who never cheats on her husband or abandons her kids
Will be living somewhere super cool, like New York City or Chicago or San Francisco
Will be making a six-figure salary with no debt, a nice house and driving a BMW
Will no longer feel the need to be perfect
Will know what love really is
Will be a member of the Junior League
Will be gearing up to run for office

Funny how the only one of those things that had happened was number seven.

Jo brushed away a lone tear that rolled down her cheek, hating herself for feeling maudlin but realizing that if she was there was probably a good reason for it.

She hadn't gone on to become Oprah's therapist, and instead of opening her own practice had decided to help out high school kids. God knew as a high school counselor she certainly wasn't making a six-figure salary, her student loan debt was mind-boggling and her dreams of owning a shiny new BMW had been replaced with the reality of driving a Ford Fusion. Mr. Right still hadn't come along, and at thirty-two she was beginning to wonder if he ever would. The only guy she'd loved as an adult had been shipped off to Afghanistan, and he'd ended things before leaving the States. And she certainly wasn't a member of the Junior League or planning on running for office any time soon. As for her current town......well, she sure hadn't pictured herself back in Del Rio taking care of her grandmother, but she supposed her adopted town of Austin was pretty cool. At least that's what people and dozens of weekly Top Ten lists always told her.

Jo continued to flip through the memory book, smiling at the photos and random pieces of high school life she'd glued to the pages. Towards the back, folded up and tucked underneath a photo of her, Jenn and Chase, was a lined piece of notebook paper, which she unfolded.

Dear Chase,

I'm sorry.

I'm sorry I haven't been talking to you much. I think I've hurt your feelings. I never meant to do that.

But I can't. I can't talk to you knowing that my mom has a thing for your dad. It's weird and gross and makes me embarrassed and ashamed.

My dad doesn't care who she sleeps with. I think the whole town knows that by now. He probably doesn't care if I sleep with someone, either.

But I'm not my mom. And I can't be around you because I'm too embarrassed and hurt and afraid you'll hate me.

You're my best friend. You, Jenn and me. We're the Three Amigos. I don't want to hurt you.

I'm so sorry.

Love,

Jo

She folded the paper back up and placed it in the book again, tucked neatly under the photo of her, Jenn and Chase. They'd been going into the ninth grade, the best of friends since elementary school. Until that awful day when Jo had overheard her mom on the phone with Chase's dad. The things her mom had said had made her hot with embarrassment and shame, and even though she didn't think Chase's dad would ever cheat on his wife, Jo still felt awful and as if it was somehow her fault. If she and Chase hadn't been such good friends, her mom might not have ever met his dad. So she'd done what seemed best to a fourteen-year-old girl—she'd distanced herself from her best friend even though it had killed her.

She'd written the note to him to try to explain, but in the end had chickened out. She couldn't. She was too embarrassed and ashamed and didn't want Chase to think she was like her mom.

Instead, she'd folded the note and tucked it into her diary. That night, after eating supper with her parents and being told not to eat so much—that "thinness is perfection!"—by the woman everyone thought of as The Easy Mom, was the first time Jo made herself throw up.

Want to keep reading? Purchase *Between the Seams* now, available at the following retailers:

Amazon | B&N | iBooks | Kobo

Want a sneak peek at the first book in Aubrey's next series?
Keep reading...

Introducing...The Texas Wranglers

Texas Wranglers rookie sensation Thomas Everett is on the path to greatness, and he's not about to let anything—especially a guarded, curvy brunette—get in his way.

Lilah Johnson's spent years trying to heal and move beyond a devastating college experience and the self-destruction that had followed in its wake. And even though she's managed (mostly) to put the past behind her, she's never quite been able to forget the one bright spot in a very dark time.

When Thomas and Lilah are thrown together to work on a fundraiser for a local nonprofit, neither of them is too thrilled with the prospect. Thomas, because he's afraid of secrets from his past being revealed, and Lilah because it's quite clear Thomas doesn't remember her at all. But when a string of covered-up sexual assaults within a local university's baseball program is uncovered, Thomas and Lilah find themselves leaning on—and opening up—to each other in ways neither of them had expected.

PROLOGUE

Five Years Ago, Stanford University

THOMAS EVERETT OPENED HIS APARTMENT DOOR AND FOUND HIS arms full of woman. From the smell of tequila, she was a very drunk woman.

His late-night inebriated visitor giggled and wrapped her hands around his biceps. Her grip was surprisingly strong, considering she could barely stand.

Jesus, what the hell was she doing wandering around by herself like this? Where were her friends? She had to have some, considering college girls always traveled in packs. Like hyenas or piranhas or something, they were rarely if ever left alone by one of their own.

She hiccuped and her grip on his arms tightened, drawing his attention to the top of her head. As he took a closer look at her, several details began to stand out to him, causing suspicion to bloom in his mind.

A quick catalogue of her appearance revealed a few important details: one, she was a redhead; two, she was about five-five; and three, she was, um, definitely on the plump side.

Apparently his teammates couldn't take "no" for an answer and brought the slumpbuster to him since he refused to go out and find one.

Assholes.

Want to know when Thomas and Lilah's story comes out? Be sure to follow me on Facebook and sign up for my newsletter to be the first to know!

About the Author

Aubrey has been reading and writing since she was about two and a half and has been an avid romance reader since she read her first romance novel in the 6th grade. She wrote her first novel in high school. It was an ~~awful~~ imaginative historical romance that involved a cross-country trip via covered wagon, and maybe some Indians. She thinks it's still on a floppy disk somewhere (DOS computer, y'all), but can't be too sure. These days, she writes contemporary romance with a lot of humor and sass and characters that have issues.

She graduated from Seton Hill University's Writing Popular Fiction program with a Master of Arts in 2008. When she's not writing, she can be found with her husband and their two dogs at home in Austin, on their ranch in west Texas, watching a football or baseball game, or with her nose stuck in a (usually virtual) book.

Connect with Aubrey:

Website | Subscribe to Newsletter | Facebook | Goodreads